DATE DUE DEC 0 6

4-3-07			
6-10			
6-30			
GAYLORD			PRINTED IN U.S.A.

CAROLINE'S JOURNAL

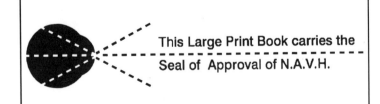

This Large Print Book carries the
Seal of Approval of N.A.V.H.

CAROLINE'S JOURNAL

KATHERINE STONE

THORNDIKE PRESS

An imprint of Thomson Gale, a part of The Thomson Corporation

THOMSON
GALE

Detroit • New York • San Francisco • New Haven, Conn. • Waterville, Maine • London

LIBRARY OF CONGRESS CATALOGING-IN-PUBLICATION DATA

Stone, Katherine, 1949–
    Caroline's journal / by Katherine Stone.
        p. cm.
    "Thorndike Press large print basic."
    ISBN 0-7862-9149-4 (lg. print : alk. paper) 1. Pregnancy — Fiction.
2. Diaries — Fiction. 3. Large type books. I. Title.
PS3569.T64134C37 2006
813'.54—dc22   2006026354

U.S. Hardcover:
ISBN 13: 978-0-7862-9149-6
ISBN 10: 0-7862-9149-4

Published in 2006 by arrangement with Harlequin Books S.A.

Printed in the United States of America on permanent paper
10 9 8 7 6 5 4 3 2 1

For Mom
Missed. Loved.
Always

There is no beautifier of complexion, or form, or behavior, like the wish to scatter joy and not pain around us.

— Ralph Waldo Emerson

PROLOGUE

Cherry Circle Drive
Seattle, Washington
December 18
9:45 p.m.
Twenty-nine years ago

The two girls sat side by side in bed, the book open on their laps.

" 'Twas the night before Christmas," the older girl began.

Seven-year-old Caroline Louisa Gallagher wasn't actually reading it. Though she could have. Every word in *A Visit from St. Nick,* and far more difficult words, too. She was an avid reader and a precocious one.

But Caroline knew this story by heart. So did her three-year-old sister. And, thanks to Caroline, Meg was learning to read.

Meg caught on right away, far more quickly than Caroline had. She was going to be a faster reader than Caroline, capable of skimming the surface — like a rock skipping on water — yet getting the meaning. Caroline's approach was more methodical. She read and considered every word.

Still, Caroline didn't foresee a future in which Meg would choose to spend Saturday mornings selecting the eight books, the library's weekly limit for young card-holders, to take home with her. Nor was Caroline's high-energy little sister likely to favor reading over the livelier pursuits that filled her days.

But at bedtime, there was nowhere Meg would rather be than curled in Caroline's bed, listening to Caroline read and gazing with her at the pictures.

Both girls loved the illustrations in *A Visit from St. Nick*. The book was new, an early Christmas present from Meg's dance teacher. Meg was the youngest in the class by several years. The older dancers received different gifts.

As Caroline recited the story's opening line, the sisters admired the drawing. The starry sky. The moonlit meadow. The pine tree sparkling with crystals of snow.

When she'd finished appreciating the scene, Meg gave a familiar, but not pushy, signal. As eager as she might've been to turn the page, she never did. She merely placed her hand at its lower corner.

It was a young hand, dimpled and small, and a ballerina's hand, graceful both in motion and at rest.

Just like Meg.

Meg's dance teacher, who was also a neighbor, had spotted the ballerina in Meg when she first began to walk. Yes, Meg toddled. As all toddlers do. But there'd been a confidence to her gait, and a lightness, as if she knew she was born to soar.

Margaret Elizabeth Gallagher spent her days soaring, and smiling, even when she was concentrating on a new step. She giggled, too, a sound as buoyant as the leaps and twirls of her graceful limbs.

Meg giggled when she accomplished choreographic challenges . . . and when she didn't. Even in defeat, Meg's happiness defied the gravity of what, for Caroline, would've been a not-so-funny failure as joyfully as her legs defied the pull of the earth.

Meg cheerfully complied with requests to perform. Such requests were frequent, especially from their parents when there was someone to impress. There'd been many "someones" in the Gallagher home tonight. Friends. Neighbors. Roger Gallagher's insurance agency employees, and, more importantly, his valued clients.

Patrice and Roger's eggnog buffet was an

annual event. And, their eldest daughter knew, an expensive one. The party cost a fortune, Caroline's mother always complained. It's worth it, her father always countered. And don't forget, he invariably added, it's a write-off.

The Yuletide buffet was a drop-by-whenever affair. Drinks would begin to flow at five.

Meg had given countless performances throughout the evening. With smiles, with giggles, and long past her bedtime.

But she'd had the energy — or perhaps simply the will — to resist the sleep her tired body wanted until after the sisters' bedtime story.

A few seconds after Meg put her hand on the page, Caroline's nod signaled that she, too, was ready to move on.

As Meg's dimpled fingers gracefully turned the page, Caroline said the words both girls knew.

"And all through the house."

Caroline's voice became a whisper with "the house," a reverent reflection of what both of them felt.

They loved the white-brick house in the picture. It was so welcoming, inviting them to wander through its forest-green door and enjoy the coziness within.

The architectural style was unlike the homes in Cherry Circle Drive. This house had two stories, not one, making it tall and square, not long and rambling.

Similar houses existed in Seattle. Caroline passed several on her way to school. She hadn't paid attention to them before. Now that she did, they looked welcoming, too. Far more welcoming than her own home.

She tried to figure out why. The two-story houses weren't decorated more grandly. The Gallaghers' seasonal decor was, in fact, the most lavish for miles.

Maybe it was just that Santa had chosen to visit such a home in their book.

Caroline didn't believe in Santa. She must have . . . once. Mustn't she? She couldn't — quite — remember. She'd certainly never embraced the fantasy as wholeheartedly, or as personally, as her little sister did. Meg regarded Santa the same way she regarded everyone she ever met: as an instant friend.

Meg was seriously considering waiting up for her friend on Christmas Eve. She'd perform her solo dance from the upcoming Christmas recital. She knew he'd like it. Then, if he wanted her to, and she couldn't imagine why he wouldn't, she'd help him deliver presents.

It hadn't occurred to Meg, although Caroline felt sure it'd occurred to *her* at Meg's age, that Santa couldn't possibly deliver presents to all the children in the world on the same night. Even if reindeer could fly, and Santa could descend — and ascend — chimneys without worrying about smoldering fires or flues left shut, there wasn't time. At ten minutes per house, and that would be fast, he'd barely be able to visit the Cherry Circle homes, much less the two-story ones, much less all of Seattle — not to mention the world.

Maybe it would never occur to Meg. Maybe for her, Santa would always be real.

Caroline hoped so. And, from the novels she read, it was a definite possibility. Whenever there were two girls in a story — and there usually were in the books Caroline chose to read — the dark-haired, dark-eyed one was serious, like Caroline. In the words of Meg's dance teacher, Mrs. Nishitani, that was how she'd "come out of the factory."

Mrs. Nishitani's observation pertained to Meg. The born ballerina. But it was true for both Gallagher sisters.

The born dancer.

The born reader.

Meg was the golden girl of the novels Caroline loved. Fearless and laughing. Caroline had searched the library's science books for proof that being a brown-eyed brunette meant you'd be serious and earthbound, and being a blue-eyed blonde guaranteed you'd believe in flying reindeer — and could yourself soar.

If the science was there, Caroline couldn't find it. Not that it mattered. She was Caroline, and Meg was Meg. They loved each other, were proud of each other. Their before-dreams storytime was as important to Meg as it was to her.

"Not a creature was stirring," Caroline said at the precise moment Meg's hand moved toward the page and Caroline nodded to show that she, too, was ready to turn to the treasures both knew awaited them inside.

The furnishings within the storybook house were as distinct from the interior design of their own home as the structures themselves. Patrice Gallagher favored sleek and modern. The book's illustrators drew fluffy and soft.

As Caroline gazed from a calico cat dozing on a sofa to a mouse sleeping peacefully within a wall, she heard a distant — yet all-too-familiar — sound.

It came from the living room, a long hallway off. But the scooping of cubes from the ice bucket was unmistakably clear. The silence that accompanied the scooping, the absence of voices, suggested that although drinks continued to flow, the guests were gone.

The silence would be broken soon enough. As successful as the party had undoubtedly been, her parents would find something to argue about.

Patrice and Roger neither screamed nor yelled. Their anger was submerged, and taut.

Caroline didn't know if Meg detected the hostility. But what she hoped, as she prepared to raise the volume of her storytelling voice, was that the only thing Meg sensed in the tinkling of ice against crystal was the promise of sleigh bells chiming in the sky.

CHAPTER ONE

Keswick Drive
Seattle
Friday, January 14
2:00 p.m.
Present Day
Darling Baby,

It's your mom — your mom! — greeting you for the first time . . . in writing that is. I welcomed you inside me three hours ago. I'm hoping — oh, I'm hoping — you'll decide to stay.

I bought this journal a week ago. I knew then (I'd known for a month) that you and I would meet this morning.

I planned to begin the journal today. But I didn't know, until I started writing, that I'd be writing to you.

I'd imagined a Dear Diary, I suppose. Or random thoughts.

But this feels right.

We're a team. Already.

Three hours is early in a pregnancy to be certain. How's that for the understatement of the century? But I *am* certain about you.

We've been trying for a while, your dad and I. Six years, two months and twenty-four days to be exact. But who's counting? We are. Obviously.

Counting and praying as we've tried the old-fashioned way *and* the newfangled ones.

Don't worry! I have no intention of sharing details of our old-fashioned attempts. I don't know how old you'll be when you read this, or if you'll ever decide to read it at all. Whatever the age, it's information you do *not* need.

What *is* relevant is that it's a new in-vitro technique, and there's a physician who's made it her specialty. Dr. Kathleen Collier isn't the reason we moved from Denver to Seattle three years ago — although she would've been reason enough had we known. *More* than reason enough.

For now, little love, we have you.

Caroline looked from the handwritten words to a cloud-covered sky. Rain would be the logical conclusion.

But there was something about this sky that made Caroline think snow. The lacy whiteness, she realized, at the edges of gray.

Meg was four when she'd identified the telltale sign, named it and explained with Meg Gallagher certainty what the laciness meant.

When the sky wore a petticoat, *this* petticoat, it was going to snow.

Caroline had never been very good at discerning the snow petticoat from other shades of white. But Meg had been unerring.

Was she seeing Meg's petticoat sky now? Or was it merely wishful thinking — as if the drifting to earth of even a single snowflake would be an indication that what she'd done was right.

Or wrong.

Caroline fought the sudden misgiving. Jeffrey would be thrilled. And he'd agree that he'd been so involved in preparing for the trial, so consumed by the myriad details demanding his attention, it was best for her to make this decision — and act upon it — without consulting him.

He'd have said yes if she'd discussed it with him — wouldn't he?

Of course he would have. He wasn't any more ready to give up than she was. His sole concern would have been her welfare. He would've been willing to risk more sadness . . . provided it was medically safe for her.

This was what Jeffrey would want.

Will want, Caroline insisted to the lace-edged sky. And he'll know it's the only choice I could have made for the eleventh embryo.

Dr. Collier's protocol called for two embryos — at blastocyst stage — per try. Over the past three years, and in couplets, the leftover embryo's ten siblings had been transferred.

And loved.

Lost.

Mourned.

For a while, in three of those five attempts, there'd been life. Seventeen days. Then twenty-two. And last summer, the possibility of joy had clung for thirty-four.

The embryos' grasp had been precarious. Cramps and bleeding gave worrisome — but not inevitable — warning that they weren't finding Caroline's womb an hospitable place to grow.

Hope drowned in a massive gush of blood a few minutes after 1:00 a.m. on a balmy August night. Jeffrey rushed her to Queen Anne Medical Center, where an emergency D & C had been required to stem the flow. Following the procedure, in the predawn hours until it was safe for her to go home, she and Jeffrey held each other — and wept.

It felt like the end.

Was the end.

Only the solitary embryo remained, and the protocol required two. Even if more eggs could be harvested, if the scarring permitted it, she'd soon be thirty-six, and with advancing maternal age, the risks increased — for mother *and* baby.

The July attempt was supposed to be their last. She and Jeffrey had known it going in. Her hemorrhagic miscarriage was merely a blood-red punctuation point. An exclamation mark, perhaps: the urgent assertion that, in addition to everything else, her very safety had become a factor.

They hadn't discussed what they already knew. And, within an hour of their return home that August morning, the loss of another woman's unborn baby had become an emotional focus for both of them.

Baby Matthew Nichols's murder — and that of his mother, Susannah — would have been consuming no matter when the crime occurred and even if Caroline's pregnancy had survived to term.

But, as forensic analysis would reveal, Caroline's miscarriage and Matthew and Susannah's murder occurred at virtually the same time. As Caroline had been reaching for Jeffrey, Susannah had been reaching, gasping, pleading, too.

Both women had fought for their unborn babies on that summer night.

And both had drowned.

For Caroline, the immersion had been warm, the spill of blood, an emotional descent.

For Susannah, the lake had been cold, the drowning real.

Caroline's assailant was invisible, a destiny against which there could be no revenge.

But Susannah's killer had a face.

And justice, for Susannah and Matthew, fell to King County prosecutor Jeffrey Wynn.

He was on call that Sunday morning. They'd been home just long enough for him to change the bloodied sheets and tuck her into bed. He'd planned to join her, to hold her while she slept and comfort her when she awakened.

It was unusual for the police to request a prosecutor's presence at a fresh crime scene. But it sent a signal. The case had the potential to be controversial, or high-profile, or political — and eventually became all three.

Caroline had watched Jeffrey's expression as he listened to words she couldn't hear.

And she'd known — without knowing details — that much as she might need Jeffrey on this Sunday morning, someone else, someone who'd died, needed him more.

She'd also known that because of her, he'd try to find a colleague to take his place. But she was fine. Not bleeding. And so groggy she'd be sleeping long after Jeffrey got home. Even before he told her what he'd learned, she'd suggested that he go.

And when he shared the detective's concern that the drowning of a pregnant twenty-eight-year-old was not the accident it was purported to be, she'd insisted on it.

The detective's assessment was a minority one. His fellow officers sensed nothing amiss.

But they were starstruck, the detective told Jeffrey. The dead woman's fiancé, and father of her unborn child, was hometown hero-turned-national-celebrity Kevin Beale. The Seattle native was following in the footsteps of football greats who had the looks — and the ability — to perform as well in front of a television camera as they'd done on the field.

Kevin Beale was early in what was predicted to be a lucrative on-air career. Since his retirement from football, the two-time Super Bowl MVP had been promoted from sideline reporting to postgame analysis at a championship pace. Just weeks before the August drownings, the rumor that had been swirling since June had been confirmed as fact. Kevin Beale would be providing televised commentary during NFL broadcasts and from the booth.

The media darling wouldn't be leaving Seattle. Not when he'd finally returned to the city that was home. He was *really* home, he told reporters with his trademark self-deprecating smile. The kid who'd always loved the water, and dreamed one day of having a canoe, had "scraped together" enough money to buy a houseboat on Lake Union.

It was beneath that houseboat that Susannah's body was found. And where, the homicide detective speculated to Jeffrey, she'd been held under water by the man who hours before and in a very public way had asked her to marry him.

During his initial encounter with the future defendant, Jeffrey concluded what the seasoned detective had. The superstar was guilty.

Proving it would be difficult. But, thanks to Susannah herself, not impossible. Her valiant but ultimately futile fight to save her baby's life had left a trail to her killer.

It wasn't much of a trail. A bread crumb here and there. The defense would attack it with the best experts money could buy. But the forensic path to the murderer was real. And, combined with the mountain of circumstantial evidence the prosecution's investigators had uncovered, a guilty verdict was — Jeffrey believed — within reach.

Jeffrey had been the prosecutor of choice in murder trials in Denver. Not the easy ones, in which the weight of the evidence tipped the scales of justice away from reasonable doubt on its own, but the cases in which circumstances and evidence had to be woven just so, creating a tapestry of truth the jury couldn't help but see.

Jeffrey had won such cases. Every one. But tough as some of those had been, *Washington v. Beale* was in a different league. Even Greg Marteen, the defense attorney, was. His record of success rivaled Jeffrey's. And, like his client, Marteen had a national following, as celebrated by court watchers as Kevin was by sports enthusiasts.

The trial would be a fight. The case already was.

There was an ugliness unlike any Jeffrey had experienced before, a no-holds-barred attempt to smear the victim, her family . . . and, in a newspaper article published November eleventh, Jeffrey's thirty-eighth birthday, the prosecutor himself.

In contrast to the patently untrue rumors about Susannah, and the false leaks about the case itself, the report about Jeffrey — and his architect wife — was absolutely correct and excruciatingly thorough: a detailed chronicling of their numerous failed attempts to conceive.

The obvious questions begged by the article became fodder for call-in radio shows, on-line bloggers and editorial correspondents on television and in print.

Had Jeffrey's personal losses clouded his legal judgement? Had he channeled his own sadness into prosecutorial zeal? Was the man who couldn't become a father jealous of the man who could? Was that why he'd charged Kevin Beale with two counts of murder one — and declined to consider lesser charges? And wasn't it interesting that Susannah's death and Caroline's most recent miscarriage occurred on the *same* August night?

It was during that November week, while, in addition to preparing the case, Jeffrey gave countless assurances of his professionalism, that Caroline made the decision about the eleventh embryo.

The decision, at least on paper, was hers to make — as all decisions about the embryos were. The granting of power of attorney to the mother was an option Kathleen Collier offered for practical reasons. The mother had to be present for the transfer. Her signed consent was easy to obtain. But a father, though equally committed to having a baby, might be on-duty overseas, away on business, at the bedside of an ailing relative in another town.

Kathleen tried to be as precise as possible — as far in advance as possible — about the date and time the transfer would take place. But a key element to the success of her technique was transferring the blastocyst at the point that most closely mimicked when it would reach the uterus had its journey started in the ovary — and when the mother-to-be's uterus was hormonally ready for implantation to occur.

The mother was on standby. The father couldn't always be.

Jeffrey had signed the power-of-attorney document without the slightest hesitation — even though, during their two years of in-vitro attempts in Denver, he'd never missed a transfer . . . and had every intention of being present in Seattle, too. For him, it had been a matter of trust, not practicality. He trusted his wife with their babies, trusted her to make the decisions that were best for them.

Until her decision about the eleventh embryo, she and Jeffrey had always discussed what to do next.

If not for Kevin Beale, they would've made this decision together, too.

The solitary embryo wouldn't be destroyed. That was a given. It could be donated to another childless couple. Snowflake babies, such embryos were called. Unique, precious gifts that found life in other women's wombs, love in other women's families.

Once Caroline and Jeffrey gave their consent — or Caroline gave it for them — the eleventh embryo could become the snowflake baby it was meant to be.

And until then? The remaining embryo lay frozen in a vault.

Held in icy limbo because its parents had yet to make the decision that must be made.

Thoughts of the lonely baby-to-be haunted Caroline. And Jeffrey, too? Caroline didn't ask. If worries about the solitary embryo weren't already tormenting him, they would the instant she suggested it.

The worries would make him sad. Sadder. And would make more difficult the impossible tasks he already faced: the pixel-by-pixel memorization of the postmortem photos of Matthew and Susannah; the heart-wrenching conversations with Susannah's family; the knowledge that there must be no prosecutorial mistake in pursuit of the conviction of Kevin Beale.

During the week when Jeffrey's personal quest to become a father became a matter of public record, Caroline scheduled an early-December appointment with Kathleen.

She told no one of her plan, and would abandon it only if she must.

Kathleen Collier didn't balk at the prospect of transferring the single remaining embryo. The protocol wasn't that rigid. Her reluctance lay elsewhere, the damage to Caroline's uterus from her multiple miscarriages and the emergency D & C a few months earlier. She needed to determine, to the extent it was possible to do so, that a baby could be carried to term, nourished to term, without undue risk of hemorrhage — and loss of life — to either mother or child.

The tests were encouraging. And today, after signing the consent that was Caroline's alone to sign, the eleventh embryo had been transferred to her womb.

Caroline looked from the snow-cloud sky to what she'd written in the journal. After a moment, she added:

You, precious snowflake. *You.*
And your dad's going to be so thrilled.

CHAPTER TWO

Motions Hearing
State of Washington v. Kevin Beale
King County Courthouse
Friday, January 14
2:30 p.m.

"There are two issues before the Court today. The first is televised trial coverage." Judge Naomi Owens glanced beyond the defense and prosecution tables to the gallery. The media had turned out in full force, and brought their attorneys with them. And, for the first time in the pretrial hearings, a television camera was — with her permission — recording the proceedings. The feed wasn't live, but snippets would be available for subsequent broadcast. "I see we have quite a bit of interest in that matter."

Judge Owens's smile was authentic. By all accounts, she was a nice human being; a loving and beloved wife, mother, sister, grandmother.

Jeffrey also knew it was a poker smile, giving no advance indication of how she planned to rule.

He'd never tried a case before her — nor had Marteen — but when *Washington v. Beale* had been assigned to her courtroom, he'd done a little research . . . and found a reputation that was, in his estimation, the best a judge could have.

No-nonsense. Fair. And, though sometimes controversial, her rulings were based on carefully reasoned principles of law. Because of that, they were invariably held up on appeal.

Jeffrey would need bold — and, in the view of the defense, controversial — rulings. Every shred of evidence, both circumstantial and certain, had to be judged admissible for the jury to hear.

In each instance, he believed, the law would support such rulings. All he had to do was present the argument flawlessly. With clarity, not emotion.

Jeffrey was emotionally invested in every case he tried. But he would've been fooling himself to pretend this case didn't have special meaning.

And special peril.

Jeffrey wasn't fooling himself. He knew he

was fighting this fight for Caroline and their lost babies every bit as much as he was fighting it for Susannah and her lost son.

He'd known, long before the question was posed in the press, that such personal involvement conferred risk. If objectivity fell by the wayside, critical mistakes could be made.

He'd weighed the risks, considered recusing himself. He would have, had he believed the case was jeopardized by his passion. It wasn't, wouldn't be. He had to be extra vigilant, that was all.

Extra mindful of the hatred he felt.

The constant vigilance was exacting a toll. Exhaustion unrelieved by sleep. Fury that grew the longer he kept it in check.

The wear and tear on him didn't matter — assuming it didn't interfere with what had to be the error-free prosecution of Kevin Beale.

It *wouldn't* interfere. Jeffrey wouldn't permit it to.

When emotion threatened, he thought of Susannah, of Matthew and, most of all, of the woman he loved.

So far, so good. Judge Owens's pretrial rulings had been favorable to the state.

But the defense was on the warpath, as evidenced by the stack of documents, on top of which Judge Owens placed her hand as she continued her introductory remarks.

"The second issue is a request from the defense that I revisit my previous rulings on the admissibility of testimony from several prosecution witnesses." Judge Owens paused to survey the pile of legal briefs before addressing the defense. "Let's deal with the second matter first. I've studied every word you've given me, Mr. Marteen."

"Thank you, Your Honor."

"My rulings stand."

"Your Honor —"

"The waivers of physician-patient and attorney-client confidentiality by Ms. Nichols's parents are legally binding. And the friends in whom Ms. Nichols confided prior to her death may, in the opinion of the Court, provide state-of-mind testimony without violating the hearsay statute. I know your client has a right to confront his accuser. In this instance, as in every case of murder, the state is doing the accusing on the victim's behalf. You're more than welcome to confront the state's witnesses. In fact, I have every confidence you'll do so aggressively — including, if you like, an attempt to overturn my rulings prior to trial. That's your prerogative. It won't hurt my feelings, nor will it affect any future rulings

I might make."

"I appreciate that, Your Honor."

"Good. Now, as regards the matter of cameras in the courtroom, I've received supportive documents from the defense and the media. I have no filings from the prosecution. The state has no position on this issue, Mr. Wynn?"

"We have conflicting positions, Your Honor."

"So you're leaving it to me to decide. That's fine. I plan to. For the record, however, please summarize the conflict for me."

Jeffrey had anticipated the request. He was prepared to offer succinct presentations on both sides of the argument. "One justification for a televised trial is the public's free and open access to the process. In this case especially, where leaks and rumors have been rampant, the opportunity for citizens to separate fact from fiction has definite benefits. Additionally, the murder of a pregnant woman —"

"Your Honor!"

"— is a public health concern."

"One moment, please, Mr. Wynn. Mr. Marteen?"

"There was no murder. My client's fiancée and their unborn son died in a tragic accident. It's an outrage for Mr. Wynn to assert my client's guilt as fact."

"It's hardly a secret that Mr. Wynn views your client as guilty. That's why we're here." Judge Owens returned to Jeffrey. "I'm assuming the public health concern you're referring to is the issue of homicide in pregnancy."

"It is, Your Honor."

"We've agreed in previous hearings that we're not going to get bogged down in a debate over how common or uncommon such homicides are. From information provided by both the defense and the prosecution, it's clear that experts could battle endlessly — and to no avail. The bottom line, as I read it, is that the necessary data has yet to be gathered. What's not in dispute is that homicide during pregnancy, and *because* of pregnancy, is a tragedy that's all too real. Given media coverage of recent cases, I'd say this is a reality the public already knows. And yet, Mr. Wynn, you're citing public health as a reason for televising the trial."

"I am, Your Honor."

"The prosecution has a case, doesn't it? You're not just using my courtroom as a classroom."

"The prosecution has a case, Your Honor,

for capital murder."

"Any other reasons to televise?"

"Not from our standpoint."

"And the reasons not to?"

The answer was obvious. Greg Marteen's indignant outburst, which would never have happened if the defense attorney hadn't seen the opportunity for a sound bite on the evening news, provided an eloquent reply.

"Cameras in the courtroom tend to prolong the trial," Jeffrey said.

"Showboating by the attorneys?" the judge suggested. With a smile, she added, "And perhaps the judge? Courtroom as classroom *is* tantalizing. We've already discussed how long both sides expect their cases to be. It's a best guess. We all know that. But let's put it on the record in the hope that'll encourage us to stick to it."

Judge Owens addressed the assembled reporters. "Jury selection starts on February fifteenth. Assuming we can get the jury impaneled in six weeks, the trial itself will begin in late March. Based on predictions both sides have made to me, the case will go to the jury in early August."

The judge turned to the defense. "If the trial is televised, Mr. Marteen, when would you anticipate jury deliberations to begin?"

"Early August, Your Honor."

"Good answer. Mr. Wynn?"

"The same, Your Honor."

"Good. I have a final question for you, Mr. Wynn. Would I be correct in assuming you've spoken with Ms. Nichols's family and they have no strong objection to a televised trial?"

"You would be correct, Your Honor. The murder of their daughter and grandson has already been a supreme invasion of privacy. Nothing that follows could be worse. And they're hopeful that in whatever manner the trial is covered, awareness of what happened to Susannah will help other pregnant women avoid similar tragedies. The proceedings will be difficult for the Nichols family, whether they're televised or not. They do understand that crime-scene and postmortem photographs will be viewed only by the jury in either case."

"That's right." Judge Owens's expression held nothing back. The penalty for leaking the photographs would be severe. After a moment, she directed her remarks to the lawyers in the gallery. "I hate to disappoint the many media advocates who've come to court expecting to give oral presentations in support of a televised trial. I've read the briefs you've submitted and find that you've adequately addressed the questions I might have had. Therefore, in the interest of demonstrating that cameras in the courtroom needn't prolong the process, I'm going to make my ruling without further ado."

Her pause was for breath, not for drama. "I'll allow a televised trial with the following proviso. A public hearing means the public hears every word. People watching from home must have the same opportunity to hear the testimony they'd have in the courtroom. Which is to say, *all* of it. Gavel to gavel."

This time, her pause was to make sure her order was sinking in. When perplexed faces told her it was, she continued. "I'm not trying to put either the networks or their legal anchors out of business. But when court's in session, commercials and commentary may occur only during sidebars, coffee breaks and lunch recess. Court will be dark on Mondays. That should allow ample time to pay the bills, rehash the past week's testimony and predict what's to come. That's the ruling, and it applies to radio and Internet broadcasts as well as TV. Failure to adhere to the parameters I've outlined will prevent the offending outlet and its affiliates from further access to the proceedings. Now," she said, "unless there's anything else, that concludes our work for today. Mr. Marteen?"

"That's all, Your Honor."

"Mr. Wynn?"

"The state has nothing more, Your Honor."

"Then I hope everyone has a nice weekend."

Judge Owens rose so quickly that a number of surprised spectators were still clambering to their feet as she exited.

Once she was gone, jubilation erupted. A televised trial was a media victory *and* a triumph for the defense. The photogenic defendant, who'd had — and might still have — a brilliant future as an on-camera personality, was a television producer's dream.

And a defense attorney's dream. Attractive clients fared better than unattractive ones, and although the only jury that was supposed to matter would be the twelve jurors themselves, public opinion had a way of seeping into the courtroom, too.

As indicated by Kevin Beale's behavior, Marteen had coached his client well. Until the room's solitary camera was shut off, his expression remained identical to the one he'd worn throughout the hearing. Attentive and solemn. When it was safe to do so, he turned to the media throng — many of whom knew him, liked him, believed him incapable of murder — and offered a grateful smile.

His gaze drifted, eventually, to the prosecutor who was attempting to ruin his life.

Jeffrey felt his gaze, and met it.

And there they were.

The father who'd prayed for babies . . . and the one who, after drowning his unborn son, returned to the warmth of his houseboat, knowing his victims were submerged beneath.

Knowing how cold they were.

And getting colder.

Jeffrey held Kevin's hate-filled gaze until Marteen wisely diverted his client's attention elsewhere. And Jeffrey thought, as he met the murderer's eyes, about another baby that was so cold.

And alone.

It wasn't fair.

None of it was fair.

Least of all asking the woman he loved to try again.

CHAPTER THREE

Highland Drive
Queen Anne Hill
Friday, January 14
3:30 p.m.

"You're a marvel, Meg Gallagher," the real estate agent raved. "But we knew that, didn't we? And I was wrong. I admit it! Your pillows are all the fluffing this house needs. I honestly thought it was so depressingly vacant the sellers would have to pay to stage it with roomfuls of furniture to make it even remotely cheerful. But, once again, your pillows have done the trick."

"I'm glad you like it," Meg said. "I hope the pillows help it sell."

"*Help* it sell? I'm predicting a full-scale bidding war within a week. Look at these ferryboats!"

The agent could have been referring to the view from the living room window. But her gaze was on the ferry-shaped pillows on the sill.

The boats weren't the only custom-made pillows in the room. A cluster of large pillows, suitable for sitting on, faced the fireplace. There were smaller pillows, too, samplers of color and fabric that suggested the kind of bold — and intriguing — decorating choices that could be made.

Meg had crafted pillows for every room in the house, each designed with the specific room in mind, splashes of color and imagination that showed prospective buyers how warm and inviting the home could be. Her creations became the property of the home-sellers who hired her services. More often than not, when purchase offers were made, the future owners specified that Meg's pillows be included in the price.

Meg called what she did "accessorizing," whether her pillows adorned empty houses or furnished ones.

Agents and sellers called it "amazing."

"They're really very easy to make," she said in response to the agent's enthusiasm for her work.

"So you say."

"It's true."

"The actual stitching may be easy, but the designs are —"

"Simple."

"— unique. Trust me, Meg. In the three years since Piper Henry's *Seattle Times* article about you, every Realtor in the area has been deluged by offers from Meg Gallagher wannabes. You have a knack. *The* knack. We're all dreading the day you realize you could make a fortune selling your pillows online. You'd only have to leave home — and change out of your bathrobe and slippers — when you *felt* like it. Doesn't that appeal to you?"

Meg managed a smile, though what she felt was terror.

She wouldn't do well with just herself as company in the rental property near Woodland Park Zoo. The one-bedroom future tear-down wasn't the problem.

She was.

It was best for her to have reasons to drive. Reasons not to drink.

And when it came to someplace she'd rather be, she'd already found it: a house abandoned by its family, waiting for a new one to take its place.

And she'd already found what she wanted to do: make such a house appear less forlorn, in the hope its emptiness would soon be filled.

"I like what I'm doing."

"That's terrific, from my standpoint. I don't want to talk you out of doing it."

"This is a great house," Meg said. "I've really enjoyed being here."

"You have a thing about colonials, don't you? Just like your sister."

"You've been to Caroline's home?"

"When it was on the market, before she and Jeffrey bought it." She smiled. "Word is that if your dream house is a colonial, Caroline Wynn's the architect for you. The style's found throughout Seattle's older neighborhoods, of course. Remember the daylight rambler you worked on for me in Woodway? The new owners are taking it down to the footprint and building a colonial designed by your sister. I saw the preliminary sketches when I was dropping off a survey map for one of the other architects in her firm. They're *sensational.* Traditional, but with interesting new touches."

"Caroline's very talented."

"I think it's a family trait. So," the agent said as, slipping her feet out of protective blue booties, she wedged them into heels that were stylish but obviously tight, "can I treat you to a latte? There's a Starbucks a few blocks away."

"Thanks, but no. I have a couple of errands to run before it snows."

The agent frowned. "It's going to *snow?* I listened to the news at noon and didn't hear anything about it."

Meg shrugged. "It's my own forecast, and it's probably wrong. The sky just has that look to it."

"I hope you're wrong. But in case you're not, I'd better get going, too."

Meg's clinic appointment wasn't for another four weeks. She didn't need to go to the medical center this afternoon. The new-patient information could "easily" be mailed, filled out and returned — as the clinic had requested — prior to February fourteenth.

In the same breath that the clinic clerk had said "easily," she'd also alluded to what was a "lengthy and really important" questionnaire. Most important was the completeness — and truthfulness — with which the patient answered. The clerk's tone indicated that the temptation to be less than forthcoming was a common one.

Meg had no doubt that candor was essential. The stakes couldn't be higher. She'd already promised herself to be unwaveringly honest. Still, it made sense to get a copy of the questionnaire as soon as possible, to get used to the idea of revealing everything she'd be required to reveal.

Picking up the questionnaire wasn't her only reason for dropping by Queen Anne Medical Center this afternoon. Nor was the fact that it was conveniently close to the house she'd just left on Highland Drive.

Today was an anniversary of sorts, the one-year commemoration of meeting the man she loved . . . the trauma surgeon who worked nearby.

Three months later, she'd told that man, that surgeon, goodbye. Over the phone. As if the farewell was of no consequence to either of them.

He'd listened in silence, hung up so quietly she hadn't realized it and, a short while later, knocked on her door.

"I love you," he'd said as he entered the house that was more a seamstress's studio than home. "I want to spend my life loving you."

"You can't want that, Mark."

He'd smiled, unworried. "Sure I can, Meg. And I do."

"But I don't." *Cannot. Do not dare.* "It's been fun. Truly. Wonderful." She'd dug deep, reverting to the party girl he'd met three months before. It wouldn't fool him. He knew the facade wasn't real. But a false shell was better than none; anything to

47

protect her from falling apart as she said the words she had to say. "You know me."

"So many men, so little time?"

"Yes."

"We blew right past your two-month rule. Don't tell me you didn't notice."

"I noticed. But with your call schedule, our actual time together was barely one month, much less three."

"What's going on, Meg? What game are you playing?"

No game, Dr. Traynor. Life and death. The very survival of my heart. "I'm not playing, Mark. I told you, it's been —"

"You don't love me. Is that what you're trying to say?"

She'd made herself look up to eyes that had darkened with desire — and glowed with love — for her. "Yes."

"I don't believe you."

"Mark," she'd whispered. "You're a great guy."

"Do not give me the you-can-do-better, you-deserve-better speech. Please. I didn't invent it, but I've perfected it. The hell of it is, I've always delivered it in good faith. I knew she *could* do better, *did* deserve better. Could and did deserve a man who loved her. You *have* a man who loves you, Meg.

And I believe I'm looking at a woman who loves me."

"There are things I haven't told you. . . ."

"Would they make me change how I feel? Not a chance. But go ahead, try me."

"I . . . can't."

"That bad?"

Yes.

"Talk to me, Meg."

"I'm really flattered —"

"Flattered?"

"— that you believe you love me."

"I do love you."

"I can't do this anymore. Let me go, Mark. Please."

He hadn't been holding her, except with his love.

But he'd heard her desperateness, and honored her plea.

Meg hadn't seen him since that April night. She'd expected to, prepared to, at a wedding in June.

And hadn't, not during the ceremony at the church, or later, in the Rainier Room at the Wind Chimes Hotel, where the reception was held.

Barring the unknowable, she'd told herself, their paths would never cross again.

Now the unknowable had happened. And, if the future unfolded as she hoped it would, she'd be visiting Queen Anne Medical Center often. This day, she'd decided, this one-year anniversary, might as well be the first of those visits.

She had to get used to being where Mark worked. The actual chance — risk — of running into him was small. The medical center was vast, the wing for new moms and their babies a substantial distance from the hospital's trauma center and emergency room.

Even if Mark had fallen in love with an ob-gyn nurse, ob-gyn doctor or the clinic clerk who'd scheduled the appointment for Meg, and even if Mark needed that new love as much as he'd once believed he needed Meg, he wouldn't wander to Labor and Delivery while on-call.

Even for love, Dr. Mark Traynor wouldn't stray more than a few racing strides from where trauma victims would arrive.

Meg could *live* in the maternity wing, and Mark would never know.

Her worry — and what, beginning this afternoon, she must practice *not* doing — was that she might wander into his domain. Just to catch a glimpse.

Just to know that his life was as happy as it should be.

As she searched for a spot in the parking

garage, Meg reflected on her definition of love. She'd thought about it a lot in the nine months since she'd last seen Mark.

The definition was quite simple. And it had stood the test of time. It was the same definition she'd believed in, and acted upon, when she was six.

Love meant caring about your loved one's happiness, your loved one's *life,* more than your own. It included a willingness to die, too . . . if, because of your dying, the beloved's happiness might be assured.

Simple. Time tested. She'd tried the dying once, and failed. The failure hadn't mattered. Her attempt had come too late. The hope for happiness had already been lost. *Killed* by her.

She'd been destined to survive. For Caroline. Not to die for Caroline, but to live for Caroline, give life for Caroline.

If, if, Caroline would let her.

CHAPTER FOUR

Keswick Drive
Friday, January 14
4:15 p.m.

It's me again. Your mom. Who knew I'd be writing you — again — so soon? Admittedly, I don't have much to report. But I have an urge to write to you that I'm not going to resist.

I've had such a *nice* afternoon, thanks to you. Puttering. Humming. Smiling. And feeling as if you're smiling, too. I'm sensing that you're happy inside me, cuddled in for a warm winter's nap.

I love that you're here.

Your dad called thirty minutes ago. On balance, he said, the motions hearing went well. The judge upheld the motions he'd hoped she would, and granted the television coverage he'd expected she might.

He's not too happy about the TV part, and accurately predicted the video clip — the grandstanding by the defense — that would be aired on the evening news. KOMO 4 has already led with it, on *First Four News* at four.

He's hoping to be home by seven. But since Greg Marteen has a habit of faxing evidentiary requests and late-breaking motions on Friday afternoons, I'm guessing it'll be closer to nine.

Whatever time he gets home tonight, I'm going to tell him about you.

I'd planned to wait for a while, to surprise him with the glorious news when you were a trimester old. But I can't wait, and I don't have to — because, with every smiling moment, I feel you're snuggled in to stay.

I'm glad I decided to keep this journal. I'd never kept one before. I must have known how right it would feel to share this joy with you.

The joy *of* you.

I'm going to write thoughts as they come, no editing allowed. The prospect's a little daunting. No second, third, tenth chances for improvement. What writing I do, e-mail included, typically undergoes a number of rewrites.

I'm not a perfectionist (your aunt Meg might beg to differ). My writing becomes (considerably!) more polished with sequential drafts.

What I write will be true. My joyful feelings. And my terrified ones. How's that for candor? I'm afraid of failing to be the mother you deserve. I love you. Already. *So much.* And I want — so much — to be the best mom ever.

Well, that's revealing, isn't it? The perfectionism I've just denied. I can't take it back. No editing allowed. And, tempting as it is, I'm not going to buy another journal and begin again.

I have to believe that most pregnant women, perfectionists or not, want to be the best moms ever. It's a lofty goal, perhaps, but a worthy one — and, from my viewpoint, the only goal a mom-to-be could have. So I'm standing by "best" as something to aspire to.

It's particularly important for me to aim high in the motherhood department. My track record, as a sort-of mother, is pretty miserable. True, I was a girl at the time, and Meg was my sister, not my daughter. But as a result of our parents' divorce, Meg and I were left to fend for ourselves. As the older by four years, it fell to me to fend for her.

Financially we were fine. Our father paid handsomely to get out of the marriage, and out of our lives. He was eager to start a new family. His next wife was waiting in the wings.

Even a medical crisis with Meg, an accidental poisoning two weeks before the divorce was final, didn't change his mind — or even delay the inevitable. All ties to his disastrous first marriage, his daughters included, were severed as planned.

Our mother didn't want us, either. But she liked the amount of child support our father was willing to pay — how much it cost *him* to persuade *her* to assume sole custody of us.

Because of the child support, and our mother's willingness to spend some of it on us, Meg and I never wanted for food, shelter, clothes.

When it came to love, we were on our own.

We weren't very good at it. Love. The consequence of being raised in a marital war zone, I suppose. The only secret Meg and I shared was the charade we maintained before the divorce — that our parents were the ideal couple and we were the picture-perfect family.

The divorce left our mother bitter, and more remote from us than ever. You'd think she would've felt relieved. *I* did. There'd never been violence in our home, but the tension between our parents was a constant source of stress.

She was bitter. Aggrieved. And either oblivious to Meg's despair, or unwilling to be bothered with it. I've always assumed it was the latter. Even our self-absorbed mother had to notice how devastated Meg was.

Meg's grief was complex. She alternated

between shell-shocked and energized, as if something could be done, must be done, to mend our fractured family. She was only six. Too young to feel relief — or anything other than the loss of her world.

Eventually she became Meg again, the remarkable little girl she'd always been. Remarkable, but not the same. She'd been a dancer from the moment she could walk. She loved dancing — until the divorce. She quit the classes that had been the highlight of her week, and refused all requests to perform.

Her dance teacher was dismayed. Our mother was incensed. But neither gentle coaxing nor relentless haranguing could induce her to reconsider . . . or offer even a glimmer of an explanation for the decision she'd made.

Caroline stopped. Had to. The emotions crammed between the lines of what she was writing demanded that she breathe. And feel. And remember the scene she'd described as "accidental poisoning."

The description was accurate. But the scene itself — she breathed deeply and let herself remember. . . .

It was the sound that awakened her, the hated tinkling of ice against crystal. But it was the middle of the night. Her mother had gone to bed hours ago. Her father was probably sleeping, too, in the apartment where he'd lived since moving out.

She got up, more curious than alarmed. The sight of Meg's open door and empty bed triggered a shiver of worry. But, she reassured herself as she followed the sound, Meg had gotten a glass of water and added ice — like her parents always did.

Just because Meg had never done that before . . .

It wasn't water Meg was drinking. Gulping. Taking bigger gulps when Caroline appeared.

"That's alcohol, Meg! *Stop.*" Caroline saw determination in the glazed eyes. When she reached for the glass, to make Meg obey her, determination became defiance . . . and anger.

"No!" Meg tried to take another swallow. Caroline's hands wouldn't let her, and the whiskey spilled, staining the recently installed carpet — a blemish that would annoy Patrice Gallagher for years to come.

"*Yes.*" Caroline claimed the glass. "Meg, what are you *doing?*"

Meg hadn't answered. She'd never answered that question. But it was obvious. She was mimicking what she'd seen her parents do countless times — and which, especially in the early evening when the girls were with them, they enjoyed. There was laughter then, and performances by Meg.

Happy times for the family on the eve of divorce.

And now, on the eve of divorce, a medical crisis for the daughter who'd been trying desperately to recall that joy.

Meg had ingested a potentially lethal amount of alcohol. It would have been lethal; she would've died on Patrice's new carpet if Caroline hadn't found her when she did, and screamed for their mother when Meg slipped into unconsciousness.

The paramedics saved her first, with intubation in the field, and there'd been heroic interventions in the ICU. Meg remained groggy for days. Then, and when she was finally discharged home, the "unfortunate incident," as Patrice referred to it, was not something Meg would discuss.

But it was the reason, ten-year-old Caroline decided, that Meg refused to dance. She *couldn't* dance. The alcohol had destroyed her perfect balance. The effect wasn't apparent from the way Meg walked. She must have discovered the damage when she tried to soar.

That was it, Caroline had thought. If only Meg would talk to her about it.

But Meg didn't need to talk about the residual effects of alcohol poisoning on her ballerina limbs. Because there were none.

Caroline saw her one day in the park, dancing as gracefully as ever. Her expression was sad. And when she realized Caroline had invaded her private stage behind the trees, the anger Caroline saw rivaled Meg's fury when she'd wrested away the glass of whiskey her sister had been drinking.

Caroline emerged from the memory with the feeling of helplessness she'd experienced on that long-ago day . . . and with a thought she hadn't had at the time. No one worried — then — about a six-year-old girl being alone in a park.

That didn't mean the danger to little girls didn't exist. Surely it had. It was awareness of the danger that had yet to surface.

Caroline shuddered at what might have happened to the solitary ballerina in the park. And she wondered if, deep down, Meg had known, even then, that it was a risky place to be. If so, it was the beginning of what would typify Meg's behavior in the ensuing years.

Recklessness that verged on danger.

And anger at Caroline's efforts to keep her safe.

With a sigh, Caroline picked up her pen and began again.

I tried to parent her. "Supervise" was the word she used the one time — we were eighteen and fourteen — she critiqued my (miserable) performance. She might choose "controlling" if asked to critique my teenage parenting today.

I don't ask. We both were there. We both know what happened.

That sounds ominous, doesn't it? As if there was something more sinister than what I've revealed.

There wasn't. Meg had no mother to speak of, and I took it upon myself to fill the void. Unfortunately, I was like a lifeguard who doubted my own ability to swim. It was safest for Meg if I never let her near the water.

Naturally, she rebelled. She was a lively mermaid. She wanted to frolic in the sea. She resented me for keeping her gasping and flailing on shore, *hated* me — a fact she made crystal-clear that day.

I'd had no idea how she felt. Yes, we'd had disagreements. But I'd believed they were tiny — albeit sharp and painful — shards that chipped off a solid rock of love.

Turns out all that was solid was Meg's wish that I disappear — hopefully "forever" — from her life.

Aaaaaaah! This is *not* what I thought I'd be writing. I'm beginning to understand why journaling as a technique for self-discovery is so frequently prescribed. It takes you places you might otherwise not go, the kind that pop into your head only to be swatted away. But once they're committed to paper — with the pledge not to revise — they demand to be followed to some sort of conclusion.

So how did I get here? Oh, yes, I segued from joyful feelings to terrified ones, and from wanting to be the best mom ever instead of the one my teenage sister and my own teenage performance forecast to be the worst.

Aunt Meg, by the way, would be a fabulous mom. *Will* be. Just as she'll be a fabulous aunt. Yes, Meg and I have that critique session in our past. And after that devastating day, I did what Meg wanted me to do. I left her, and her city.

Left Meg, Caroline reflected. And Seattle. And stayed away.
And stayed away.

I honored Meg's wishes for fifteen years.
Three years ago, the man who'll be your

dad told me he'd been looking into a job in Seattle. The prosecutor's office was in the market for someone with expertise in homicide trials, and he thought he might apply — assuming I'd be willing to go with him if he got the job.

He said this casually, knowing that for me it wasn't casual at all. And, of course, he was doing it *for* me. He knew I'd forever regret not trying to reconcile with my sister.

A few months later, after an exchange of e-mails, Meg and I met at the University Village Starbucks.

Within seconds of seeing her, I blurted out the "I'm sorry" that was supposed to have been the preamble to the lengthy apology I'd rehearsed. Meg didn't even want the preamble. She shook her head, waved my *sorry* away, said she was sorry, too.

That was it, and it was enough, a hasty acknowledgment of our best-forgotten past and (I think) a willingness to move on.

I think, Caroline mused.

The truth was, she didn't really know how Meg felt.

In the three years since her return to Seattle, she and Meg had been on their best behavior with each other.

Neither wanted conflict. Whether both

wanted closeness — Caroline did — wasn't so clear.

In the beginning, there'd been no allusions whatsoever to their past. Eventually, there'd been a glancing one. Their mother. According to Meg, she was alive and flourishing with her rich new husband in their California home. The source of Meg's information remained vague. The Internet, perhaps. She hadn't spoken to their mother since Patrice had moved away when Meg was eighteen. And, like Caroline, Meg had no more interest in reconnecting with Patrice than with the father who'd left when they were girls.

Eventually, because it was such a huge part of her life, Caroline had shared her attempts to have a baby. She'd been fearful of the revelation; afraid that although politeness might control injudicious words, Meg's expression would be revealing. You want to be a mother? *You?*

But even the most paranoid scrutiny of Meg's beautiful face had failed to discern disapproval. This intensely personal topic had become, in fact, one they comfortably shared. Meg knew of the Reproductive Medicine Clinic, and of Kathleen Collier, too. There'd been newspaper articles about both. She said she was glad that was where

Caroline was getting her care. She seemed truly hopeful that, with Kathleen's expertise, Caroline and Jeffrey would have the baby Meg *seemed* to believe they should have.

All of that was good. So good an outside observer might conclude that Caroline's "I think" and its tentativeness could be abandoned.

But Caroline had been blindsided once by Meg. Yes, it had been in the past. But the memory ran as deep as the hatred that had erupted from Meg on that long-ago day.

I was the prime mover in our reunion. It was my move to make. I'd been the controlling — and unauthorized — mother when we were girls.

I don't know if Meg would ever have tried to contact me. And, I've told myself, I don't ever need to know. But it hurts to think she might not have. It's one of those thoughts I try to block before it surfaces. I feel it coming as a sadness before it forms a coherent thought — and I force it away.

I'm still the prime mover. I call Meg more often than she calls me.

We don't make an event of birthdays (we phone each other, send cheery e-mails), and, although we've invited her to join us for our Christmases in Denver with your dad's family, she's always declined.

I've assumed she's had plans with friends.

I hope so — if that's what she wants.

I do know how she spent many days and hours of this Christmas. A client told me. Yesterday. The client, Laura Dole, is a volunteer at Children's Hospital. She said I should've seen all the stuffed animals Meg made for the sick kids there. She added, quickly, that undoubtedly I *had* seen them all.

I hadn't, of course. I was aware that Meg made many-shaped pillows — trees, Space Needles, sailboats — for her houses. But I had no idea she made stuffed animals, too . . . or that she spent Christmas Eve going from sickbed to sickbed giving them away . . . or, as Laura told me, that the children's faces radiated pure wonder when she did.

I've been thinking I should tell Meg what I heard from Laura. That sounds, doesn't it, like something that shouldn't require a moment's thought?

But even as a girl — after the divorce — Meg didn't like hearing nice things about herself. Especially when the compliment came from me.

She's still pretty resistant to compliments. They unsettle her somehow. Make her uneasy. And, therefore, make me uneasy, too.

But maybe my uneasiness stems from the

fear that, if I push her, she'll lash back with something I *don't* want to hear . . . as she did, once, years ago.

And maybe it's time, on this day of new beginnings, for me to become a little bolder.

CHAPTER FIVE

Queen Anne Medical Center
Trauma Room Seven
Friday, January 14
4:40 p.m.

The trauma room wasn't the scene of the tragedy. Or of the crime. That bloody site was two miles north, at a convenience store on Highway 99.

By now, sixteen hours after the carnage, the store was probably sparkling clean — like the trauma room where Mark was standing — the bullet holes covered, the blood washed away.

There'd been much blood at the crime scene. And, despite the best efforts of first-responders and civilians alike, more had been lost en route to the hospital. The paramedics had staunched what arterial bleeding could be subdued, and the van had sped through the midnight traffic at the fastest pace that was safe, and every driver in the van's racing path had heeded the sirens and pulled aside.

After it was all over, after all was lost, the police who'd escorted the van confirmed to Mark the compliance of every citizen involved. It was undoubtedly the truth. The cops had no reason to sugarcoat the facts. And, Mark knew, their fury and frustration at the senselessness of what had happened rivaled his.

Everyone in the field had done exactly what was required of him or her. And when the victim reached the trauma center? To an inexperienced observer, the activity might have appeared chaotic. In truth, it was elegantly choreographed and meticulously rehearsed — in anticipation of catastrophically injured human beings like the young woman who'd needed their help sixteen hours ago.

Each highly trained participant had predetermined tasks, known and practiced in advance. And last night, as on every night in Mark's experience at Queen Anne Medical Center, each had performed flawlessly.

But, he thought as he surveyed the room where the woman had died, the best trauma team he'd ever worked with hadn't been enough.

"Hey, Mark."

He recognized the voice without turning around. Dr. Rachel Blair was one of the exceptional health care professionals who'd done her job flawlessly — and to no avail. Rachel had been the anesthesiologist on call.

The twenty-two-year-old victim hadn't been their first patient of the night, or their last. But she had the distinction of being the patient who had died.

"Hey, Rachel."

"Long day."

She meant emotionally long. But the hours had also added up. They'd begun their twenty-four hours in the hospital at eight yesterday morning, and were off, in theory, at eight today.

A 7:00 a.m. arrival had required six and a half hours of ultimately successful surgery — enabled by expert anesthesia. The patient had since been transferred to the intensivists in the ICU.

"Long day," Mark agreed.

"You should go home."

"You, too,"

There'd been a time when Mark and Rachel would've gone home, to her place, together. They'd been lovers before he met Meg . . . when he met Meg. They'd almost become lovers again, four months after he and Meg had parted.

It had been a night like tonight would be, when Mark was angry with fate, and with himself for not having been able to do more.

On such a night, sex was a welcome escape.

He'd made it to Rachel's front door, and no further. The unfairness to Rachel should've been enough to stop him. He liked to think it would've been, if the memory of Meg hadn't already intervened.

"Mark?" Rachel's voice, now, sounded like it had on that summer night. Her expression, too, was the same. She knew about Meg. But she was willing to, wanted to, sleep with him anyway.

Mark's smile, now as then, was gentle. "Have a good weekend, Rachel. I'll see you Monday."

Mark walked outside, into the chill twilight air. Instead of going to his car, he veered toward a terrace beyond the emergency room.

The terrace was unlighted, and small. An architectural afterthought of limited value — except to the lovers who'd discovered it a year ago.

It had become their private place, his and Meg's, when he was on call. She'd drop by

70

the trauma center lounge, and chat with whoever was having coffee, until Mark was free. They'd go to the terrace then, oblivious to the elements, warmed by their love, and they'd touch, and talk and enjoy the view.

The city was magnificent on this winter night, its lights sparkling in the cold.

Meg would love the sparkles, he thought.

Meg. Meg.

Meg . . . who didn't want him, but to whom he'd been faithful for nine months, and counting.

Before falling in love with Meg, the notion of his choosing abstinence over no-strings sex would've come as *quite* a surprise. More surprising was the falling in love.

He'd been a loner all his life. Social? Yes. Sexual? Absolutely.

But, at his essence, he was a man who preferred to go to sleep alone, wake up alone, live alone.

That was who he was, and he'd come by it honestly.

Mark was the lust-child of a married man and the secretary who'd believed her boss would leave his wife and three sons for her. The rude awakening, which coincided with her telling Stephen Traynor she was pregnant, was ultimately made palatable by the enormous amount of money Stephen paid her for leaving town — and, assuming she decided to have the baby, for keeping its paternity a secret.

Once she and the money were where she wanted to be, she arranged for her one-month-old son, accompanied by legal documents relinquishing her maternal rights, to be delivered — by nanny — to the Traynors' upscale Chicago home.

The midafternoon delivery was carefully timed. Stephen Traynor's ex-secretary knew when Angela Traynor tore herself away from the tennis club to greet her three boys — ages nine, eleven, twelve — on their return from school. The delivery was also witnessed by neighbors, colleagues and, shortly after it was made, by Stephen himself. Anonymous messages left by the baby's mother saw to that.

Something big would be happening at the Traynor home, she said. An impromptu party. Join the fun.

The illegitimate son couldn't be put up for adoption. Not when everyone knew. The living symbol of an infidelity that had nearly destroyed his family was accepted, though not welcomed, into their home. Cared for by hired help, Mark was viewed as invisible by his relatives — and his stepmother. So invisible they never bothered being cruel.

He was fine on his own. Did fine. And, as he grew into a very handsome teenager, with a very healthy sex drive, the loner became social. And remained social.

His life, when he met Meg, was good. Terrific. He loved his work, enjoyed relationships of pleasure and friendship with women, liked waking up alone.

He hadn't realized, until Meg, that he'd been lonely all his life.

Mark was acutely aware of what loneliness felt like now. He'd been living it every minute of every day — and every night — without her.

Meg detoured, too, before going to her car.

The terrace would beckon to her until she saw it one last time. This wintry evening, when it was sure to be empty, was an excellent occasion to do so.

He was facing away from her, staring at the city lights below.

She saw, in his weighted silhouette, the frustration and sadness he'd permitted her — and only her — to see.

She'd learned, over coffee in the trauma center lounge, about the stress suffered by those who worked in emergency settings.

Trauma personnel could witness as much death in a single shift as most people see in a lifetime.

It was a particular kind of death. Unexpected. Accidental. Random. Sometimes violent.

The survivors had no chance to say goodbye.

They screamed their despair to the physicians and nurses who'd done their best to save the child who'd toddled into a neighbor's pool, the brother who'd been felled by shots fired in a mall, the mother who, on her way home from the grocery store, was killed by a teenager driving drunk. . . .

Burnout among trauma personnel was frequent. And understandable.

Meg knew Mark wouldn't burn out.

But she worried about the burning in, the damage to his soul from the daily tragedies he could neither prevent nor control.

She approached with footsteps so light he didn't hear.

"What happened?" she asked, as if they'd walked together from trauma center to terrace — and had not, nine months ago, said goodbye.

"Meg," he whispered. Meg. Meg. *Meg.* Then he turned. "Hi."

"Hi."

"How are you?"

"Good. You?"

I miss the woman I love. He didn't say it. His problem, not hers. "Never better."

"*Ha.* What happened?" she asked again.

"Somebody decided a human life was worth ten dollars and change."

"If you couldn't save him or her —"

"Her."

"— she couldn't be saved."

"It was a matter of *seconds,* Meg. If she'd lost even a cc less of blood before she got here . . ."

"I'm sorry."

"So am I."

Silence fell. And with it, a shared recognition of where they were, and how cold it was. It had never felt this cold before. Even on nights when the thermometer said it was colder.

"Well," she murmured. "I'd better get going."

"Earlier, when I got out of surgery, I caught a glimpse outside. I wondered if it was your petticoat sky."

The night air might have been warmed by his memory of what she'd told when they'd been together. When they'd loved each other.

But the air Meg inhaled before answering

had become colder still. "Yes."

"So it's going to snow?"

"I think so." Meg paused without inhaling. "Well. I'd better —" *leave you.*

"Do you have plans for this weekend? We always said we'd spend a snowy weekend together."

"Yes. We did. But I . . . can't."

"Won't."

"I have plans."

"Ah. Anyone I know?"

Meg envisioned her final errand for today, a shopping spree as premeditated as her clinic visit had been. "Johnny Walker. Jim Beam."

"You're spending the weekend drinking?"

"And sewing."

"Alone?"

"I do my best sewing alone."

"And drinking alone?"

Oh, yes. "That, too. Don't worry, Mark. I don't drink and drive."

"I didn't imagine you would. That's not what's worrying me."

"Nothing should be worrying you. Nothing about me. Alcohol and I are good friends. Old friends. Just because you've never seen me drink . . ."

"I have seen you drink, Meg."

There could only have been one time, one

place. Last June, in the Rainier Room at the Wind Chimes Hotel. He must've been there after all.

"You were at Piper and Richard's reception?"

"Why wouldn't I have been?"

"It's just . . . I didn't see you at the church. I thought maybe you were on call."

"I'd been on call the night before. I had a few things to finish up, so I missed the ceremony, but made it to the reception. I'm flattered you looked for me at the church."

Flattered had an edge, reminding her she'd said she was "flattered" that he believed he loved her. Was it a test? To see if she remembered?

As if she could ever forget any words — any moments — they'd shared.

But had she?

"You were at the reception," she repeated softly.

"You don't remember seeing me."

"No. As you've already pointed out, I was drinking. The evening's a bit of a blur."

"How much of a blur?"

"After a certain point, pretty complete."

"You're serious."

"Why? Did I do something I shouldn't have? And don't say 'You tell me.' We've already established that I don't remember."

"Tell me what you do remember."

"Why?"

"Why not?"

Because if I do, you'll think less of me . . . and stop looking at me as if you miss me and want me and — and, Meg told herself, *that* was the point.

"Okay," she said. "I remember the wedding. It was very beautiful. Everything Piper hoped it would be. The reception was, too. What I remember of it. The decorations were elegant, and fragrant. White roses. And the champagne flowed. I had a flute or two as I made my way to the dance floor. And more — waiters kept appearing — while I listened to the band. That's what I wanted to do. Listen to the band. Piper was thrilled that Phil Kirby was playing. His guitar solos were so emotional, she said. Touched you deep inside. I remember thinking she was right, and that I was happy standing where I was, listening to him play. And, I guess, drinking champagne. My memory falters after that. I suppose I listened to his music and sipped — too much — champagne."

"You danced."

No. It wasn't just her lungs that filled with ice. Her entire being did. "I wouldn't have danced." I *don't* dance.

"You did."

She searched for a glimpse of a memory. And found darkness. She'd drunk to the point of amnesia. Apparently she'd forgotten that even the idea of dancing made her ache. More than forgotten, apparently. Indulged.

"Naked and stumbling?" she managed to ask.

"Clothed and beautifully."

"But you could tell I'd been drinking."

"You were drinking while you danced."

"Would you have been able to tell I'd been drinking if you hadn't *seen* me drink?"

Mark had been asking himself the same thing. The simple answer was no. She hadn't appeared impaired during the twenty minutes between when he arrived at the reception and she left. The single glass of champagne he'd watched her swallow certainly hadn't caused alarm. True, when they'd been together, she'd invariably declined so much as a glass of wine. But, more often than not, so did he.

Until now, it hadn't occurred to him that what had troubled him that night had anything to do with how much alcohol she'd consumed.

He *had* been troubled, though. Deeply concerned about the woman who, to admirers on and off the dance floor, was enchantment in motion . . . but who, to the man who loved her, seemed sad, even as she smiled.

And alone, despite the crowd of men surrounding her. She danced with all of them, and none of them.

Her mind was elsewhere, as was her gaze.

Was she looking for him? Mark had wondered.

No. He was easily seen. What Meg was searching for was far away . . . somewhere that didn't exist.

Not for her.

"Mark?"

He gave her the simple answer. "No. I wouldn't have been able to tell you'd been drinking. You hid it, handled it, very well."

Dangerously well. Mark knew that — now. Meg's ability to appear unintoxicated when her blood alcohol level was many times the legal limit indicated a significant and long-standing familiarity with alcohol.

"You said you and alcohol are old friends?"

"We met when I was six. It wasn't a good experience. But it wasn't bad enough to stop me from trying again when I was fourteen."

"Have you had memory losses before?"

"How would I know? I told you, I do my

best drinking alone." Her flip remark wasn't well-received by his dead-serious eyes. "There's no way for me to know, Mark. I can tell you that the pillows I make while I'm drinking always turn out how I intended them to."

It wasn't reassuring. Mark had already determined that her motor skills were unaffected by large amounts of liquor.

"For some reason," he said, "you drank a lot that night."

You know why! I thought I'd be seeing you. That was why she'd had the evening's first two drinks — vodka — before leaving home. "It was an . . . unusual night. I'd been working hard. I hadn't slept much, or eaten much. But when I'd finished everything I needed to, and knew I was going to make it to the wedding, I was in the mood to celebrate. I guess I went a little overboard. I must've suspected I would, because I'd planned accordingly. I'd hired a car and driver for the evening, and got home safe and sound. I was celebrating, Mark! Don't look so worried." So *caring.*

"Why do you drink?"

"For the same reason *you* do, Doctor, when you're not on-call and won't be driving. There's all that medical data, you know.

The science that shows alcohol's good for the heart."

"For some hearts, Meg. Many hearts. But only in moderation, and for its medical effects . . . not its emotional ones."

"You've concluded that I'm an emotional drinker?"

"Haven't you just told me you are?"

"It's not a big deal. So I feel like escaping — and celebrating — once in a while. Doesn't everyone?"

"We're not talking about everyone, Meg. We're talking about you."

"Let's not."

Mark remained undeterred. "Did you drink when we were together? When you were alone and I was on call?"

She could tell him yes, and that would be that — wouldn't it? He'd be relieved their relationship had ended when it did, for as serious as *they* had seemed, her relationship with alcohol had been more important. Maybe the lie would accomplish what the truth had not. He'd be disgusted . . . and he'd stop looking as if he wanted to pull her close and never let her go.

Of course she didn't drink when they were together. She'd wanted nothing to blur the joy.

Would the lie disgust him? Perhaps. But it

might hurt him, too. Meg knew the pain of discovering that the people she loved drank and drank and drank in an effort to endure the hardship of enduring *her*.

She'd never inflict such unhappiness on Mark.

"No," she finally said. "I didn't drink when we were together. Never. But really Mark, a glass or two of Scotch is not a big deal."

"Your plan to spend the weekend drinking is."

"A few drinks! And, for the record, they'll be my final few."

"You're quitting?"

"I'm stopping for a while."

"How long?"

Meg shrugged. "A year, maybe longer."

"Can you do that?"

"Of course I can. And I will. I have a 7:00 a.m. appointment with an agent Monday morning. I'll be sober for hours before I make the drive."

"But you'll be drinking from now until Sunday."

"*A few drinks.* It's what I want to do, Mark. What I choose to do."

"Fine."

"Thank you!"

"Let's do it together."

"Drink?"

"Drink. Talk. Whatever you want."

Meg imagined the joy of saying hello again and felt the ache of saying goodbye. She might have willingly paid the price — except that the snowy weekend of love Mark was suggesting couldn't happen. "I'm afraid you'd be disappointed," she said.

"I'm not."

"We wouldn't be able to do what *you* want . . . what we did best."

The muscles in Mark's jaw tightened. A tautness, Meg soon discovered, that was nothing compared to his voice.

"What we did best, Meg, was love each other."

She looked away. Then forced herself to once again meet his eyes. "We couldn't make love."

"Fine."

"Would you like me to tell you why?"

"Sure."

"Caroline miscarried in August."

"I know," he said softly. "I'm sorry."

"You know? Oh, the leak to the media."

"I was in the E.R. the night Caroline came in. Her pressure was low. I helped with the IV."

"She never told me."

"I'm not sure she was aware it was me."

"Thank you. For finding a vein."

"Anytime. How's she doing?"

"She doesn't talk about it. Not to me. But I think she and Jeffrey have reached the end of what they can do, what's safe for Caroline to do."

"Caroline's the reason we couldn't make love this weekend?"

"Yes."

"And why you won't be drinking . . . for a while. You're going to have Caroline's baby for her."

"I'd like to. I've just picked up the information packet from the Surrogacy Center at the Reproductive Medicine Clinic. My initial appointment's in a month, and there'll be another month of tests after that. But," she said, "about the time a jury's impaneled in the case against Kevin Beale, I should find out whether I qualify to be a surrogate."

"Why wouldn't you qualify?"

"You have to be psychologically capable of carrying another woman's baby."

The man, the physician, who'd just correctly diagnosed her as having emotional reasons for excessive drinking, should have nodded solemnly. He might even have added, You're right, Meg. That could be an issue.

Instead, and without the slightest hesitation, he said, "No problem there."

"And physically capable."

"Is there something that makes you doubt you would be?"

"No," she said quickly. "Not that I know of. I guess I'll find out. And, assuming it's all okay, the longer I've been abstinent from . . . everything, the sooner it would be safe to do the in vitro."

"Caroline and Jeffrey must be so grateful."

"They don't know, Mark. And I don't want them to. I want to be certain the clinic gives me the go-ahead first. Dr. Collier doesn't know, either. The physician I'll be seeing at the Surrogacy Clinic is someone else."

"I won't tell anyone."

"Thank you."

"Meg?"

She saw the question — the invitation — in his dark green eyes. Despite everything she'd just told him, he wanted to spend a snowy weekend with her.

Meg saw the love. And the longing. And . . .

"I can't, Mark." *I can't.*

The regret in her tone was mirrored in her face. And in both, Mark also detected her fear — *of us,* he thought. Of our love.

And, most of all, he now knew, of herself.

"Okay," he conceded gently. "But one last thing."

"Yes?" Her voice was wary.

"You're giving up alcohol for Caroline. For a year, you said, maybe longer. What I'm wondering, Meg, is whether you've ever considered giving up alcohol for *you.*"

CHAPTER SIX

Caroline worried a little about the voice message she'd left for Meg, the ending in particular.

She'd begun as usual, with a cheery hello and the hope that all was well with Meg. She and Jeffrey, she said, were fine. There'd be cameras in the courtroom, she added, as Meg had probably already heard.

Then, as if the memory had just come to her, she'd said, "I was talking to Laura Dole the other day. I'm designing their new home. She raved about the stuffed animals you made for patients at Children's Hospital this Christmas. Every one of them, Laura said, made a huge difference in a sick child's life. She was very appreciative, and hoped you knew that, but whenever she thanked you, you shrugged it off. I promised her I'd tell you, too."

That part of the message was good, Caroline decided. She'd referred to Meg's stuffed-animal-making as if it were something she and Meg had discussed, not something she'd learned about accidentally. And when it came to Meg's kindness in donating the animals, she attributed the raves and the admiration to Laura rather than herself.

Saying how terrific she, too, thought it was would've been too much too soon.

But her boldness, in celebration of new beginnings, prompted her to finish the message with words she would've edited — deleted — had she considered them in advance.

"Have a great weekend," she'd said. "I've been looking at the sky, thinking it's going to snow. I may be way off. You were the only one who could ever really tell."

She'd ended the message there, in the territory of their past, where she'd made such a concerted effort not to tread. At least she'd hung up before asking "What do you think?" — which Meg would've felt obliged to answer.

By 10:00 p.m., when Jeffrey pulled into the driveway, the snow-sky issue was moot. His headlights illuminated the flakes that had been falling for an hour, and would blanket the city throughout the night.

Caroline met him in the garage.

He looked so tired, and it was only going to get worse between now and the day, six months hence, when the jury would render its verdict. Despite Judge Owens's refusal to overturn her previous rulings — thus clearing the way for testimony Jeffrey considered crucial to his case — the smile Caroline saw was more worried than victorious. Already anticipating next week's pretrial battles, she supposed, the ones her exhausted husband would spend the weekend preparing.

It was a loving smile, too, and when they were close enough to touch, they kissed, before walking into their home.

When they reached the family room, Jeffrey set his briefcase on the floor and hung his coat in a nearby closet. The room was where they relaxed at day's end, and shared the pieces of their lives the other had missed.

Caroline began by filling him in on the coverage of today's hearing. It had made the news, both locally and nationally and, in some instances, was discussed at length.

"Every network showed *the* clip. Greta van Susteren's panel on Fox instantly saw it for the silliness it was. Bernie even suggested that Marteen was simply testing the lighting in Judge Owens's courtroom, so he could get his 'image people' on it if he didn't look as fabulous as he should."

Jeffrey laughed. "I love Bernie. He's probably dead-on."

"Greta was dead-on when she commented that it was going to be a pretty camera-friendly front row — you, Marteen, Beale. However, in the interests of being fair and balanced, she didn't state what was patently true."

Caroline didn't state it, either. She merely smiled at her very handsome husband.

"You're a little biased."

"I'm a *lot* biased. I'm also right. In addition to being the most gorgeous, you're also the only one who looks serious, intelligent, *not* guilty, *not* sleazy, *not* willing to say whatever it takes to win the case. I've decided it's all for the best that the trial's being televised. Viewers will hear the truth, and see it presented by someone they trust."

"I hope so. Any comments on the judge's gavel-to-gavel stipulation?"

"Everyone's jumping onboard, saying that's how televised trial coverage *should* be."

"No argument there."

"Oh, and KOMO's lined up James Gannon to do their expert commentary."

"That's good," Jeffrey said. "Really good. How was your day?"

"Good," she echoed softly. "Really good.

At least I think so. Hope so."

"It sounded definite a minute ago."

"I know. But, suddenly, I'm uncertain."

"About?"

"A decision I made."

Jeffrey exhaled as he whispered, as if he'd been punched before the breath. "The embryo."

"Yes. At the time it felt all right not to discuss it with you. It would've been another worry, another decision —"

"It's your decision to make, Caroline. That's what we agreed."

Caroline looked at exhausted eyes, more gray than blue as the man she loved tried to conceal from her his deepest — darkest — thoughts.

But he couldn't hide the obvious.

"Jeffrey. I'm sorry. I *should* have discussed it with you. I was afraid you'd try to convince me not to go through with it. But I *had* to."

"It's a generous decision, Caroline."

"Generous? Oh," she murmured. "You think I donated the embryo to someone else?"

"Didn't you?"

"No. I couldn't."

"So what decision did you make?"

"To try again."

"Only if it's safe for you."

Caroline felt the smile from deep inside. After a moment it reached her face. "It is safe, Jeffrey. You know how cautious Kathleen is. It is safe. *Was* safe."

"Caroline?"

"The transfer was this morning. And," she whispered, "I already feel our baby inside me."

His closed mouth trapped an unspoken emotion. His throat swallowed it. But he was hoarse when he spoke. "That's not possible."

"I know."

"You don't look as if you know."

"How do I look?"

"Radiant."

"*See?* I'm not crazy. I promise. It really does feel different, Jeffrey. *I* feel different. And I feel her — or him — as a presence inside me. I'm *not* crazy, though I realize it might sound that way. I'm fine." She stared into his eyes. "Is this okay? This decision I made? Is it what you would've decided, too?"

"You know it is."

"Good," she whispered.

"Really good," he agreed, pulling her close.

As they held each other, swaying gently,

Caroline wondered if he sensed what she did, that it wasn't just the two of them in the embrace.

Not just the two of them . . . ever again.

"And safe?" he asked again, as they swayed.

"So safe," she vowed. "For the baby. And me."

CHAPTER SEVEN

It was snowing, too, when Meg parked in front of her Woodland Park rental.

As ready as she'd been to numb herself to the ache of seeing Mark, she'd forced herself to wait.

And wait.

She'd *gotten* the alcohol right away. Champagne, not hard liquor, selected the way she would've selected the Scotch or bourbon, the most cost effective in terms of price per ounce.

Instead of driving home, she'd gone to one of the fabric stores she frequented. The inventory was ever changing, and there were manager's discounts on Friday nights. She was between houses. But she made purchases nonetheless. When she spotted fabric she liked, she bought it. Sooner or later, it would find its way into an empty house.

She'd spent several hours in the store and, once home, unloaded the fabric before the champagne.

She was behaving like a dieter before a new diet, she supposed. Tormenting herself before indulging in the final binge, the excess that would leave her feeling so physically ill — and feeling such emotional self-loathing — that Monday morning and its restrictions would be a welcome relief.

Dieters probably gave themselves pep talks during the final indulgent weekend, promises that this was *it,* they'd lose the weight and keep it off forever. Yes, it meant a change of lifestyle: a new relationship with food, coupled with a truce between who they wanted to be and the self-destructiveness that compelled them to eat.

Meg had never been overweight.

Food, to her, was fuel.

She'd also never smoked.

Maybe smokers splurged, too, before they quit — pack after pack in rapid succession, punishing their lungs one last time.

Meg's poison was alcohol.

Her poison, and her medication.

Yes, Mark was right. She didn't drink for medicinal value. But she took her alcohol like medicine. Methodically, and hurriedly, without paying any attention to fragrance, color, temperature, taste.

And, since age six, she never used ice.

She could try savoring the champagne on the snowy weekend that lay before her. She didn't *have* to rush. There was ample time to drink her fill.

Maybe she'd try a little savoring as the weekend wore on.

For now, she poured as much champagne as possible into the largest glass she had. With the room-temperature bottle of champagne in hand, she settled into a living-room chair and watched the falling snow.

She had yet to take the first soothing swallow. She put it off a little longer, in a negotiation with herself. She could begin to drink whenever she pleased. But once she did, she had to think about Mark — and the love, a love that started at an engagement party on this very night a year ago. . . .

Piper Henry, the bride-to-be, was the *Seattle Times* reporter whose article on Meg's business had launched numerous imitators. How hard could it be to make pillows and toss them hither and yon in an empty house?

The article had also expanded Meg's real estate agent clientele, and made it easy for Caroline, in Denver, to find Meg's e-mail address on-line.

Piper would've written the article no matter who the pillow maven had been. She specialized in local interest stories, the housing market being a recurrent one.

Meg's role in selling houses was worthy of an article. But there was added interest for Piper, because of Meg herself. It would be the second piece Piper had done on Meg. The first had been years before, in high school, when Patrice Gallagher's marriage to a wealthy older man had meant a relocation to a Hunt's Point mansion, and a new high school for Meg.

A junior-year transfer student could have been invisible. The school was large. Its most coveted clique, the *popular* teens, had been established — and had been impenetrable — since middle school.

By junior year, everyone who cared about being part of a group had found one . . . or created a group of their own.

Meg had never been a joiner. Even when the in-crowd indicated it would toss tradition to the winds and welcome her with open arms, she declined.

She liked her circle of one. She had less choice about being invisible. She couldn't be. Not as long as she was Meg.

She radiated what every teenager yearned for — confidence in who she was. The radiance began at her flawless skin, and glowed outward. She draped her slender body in daring mixes and matches of fabric, and braided more color — flowers, ribbons, beads — into her long golden hair. She smiled at everyone, afraid of no one.

Afraid, her admiring classmates concluded, of nothing at all.

She was invited to every party. On occasion, she went. She was also pursued by every teenage boy who had the courage to do so. As a result, her two-month rule became known to the entire school.

The longest she'd ever date anyone — senior class president Will Keeling included — was two months. It would be an intense two months. Plenty of time to learn the best of what there was to know.

As editor of the school paper, Piper Henry was a student member of the cheerleading selection committee. She'd never spoken to Meg. But she'd heard all about her, including the fact that no one had ever seen Meg dance — much less cheer — or spend more than a few minutes at a football game.

But Meg was trying out for the cheerleading team. Her performance, while more ballet than gymnastics, won her a unanimous vote on the first ballot. Her influence on the team could be substantial, the selection committee agreed. There was little doubt the five other girls would follow her lead.

Piper's interview with Meg took place ninety minutes after the six cheerleaders, plus one alternate, were announced. During the interview, Meg made an announcement of her own. On reflection, she'd decided not to do cheerleading after all. Too much of a commitment, she said.

The explanation was credible, coming from the free spirit with the two-month rule. No one questioned it. Not even Piper, at the time. Later, the real reason dawned crystal clear.

With Meg out, the alternate made the team. Being a cheerleader would mean the world to that seventh-place girl.

And Meg Gallagher already had the world.

Piper's *Seattle Times* article, "Pillow Talk," started on the front page of the real estate section and spilled over to the next. It was longer than Piper's editor had envisioned. But every word made it to print.

Piper chronicled the work experiences that culminated in Meg's becoming the sole proprietor of a small business that was indisputably unique — and, from the vantage point of Meg's coworkers and clients in the numerous jobs she'd previously held, made perfect sense.

Meg never stayed at one job very long, as

if she had a rule about that, too. But from her barista days at Starbucks, to waitressing at Ivar's, to the aerobics classes she'd given at a local gym, she inevitably made bold, unexpected, colorful embellishments to the environment.

She started making pillows at about the same time she became a personal shopper at Nordstrom. When a real estate agent client admired the dressing-room pillows, and learned that Meg had made them, she asked Meg to "take a peek" at a house she was trying to sell. The home was furnished but drab. With minimal expense, and lots of vision, it was transformed by Meg.

A "nonsurgical face-lift," the agent who'd "discovered" her was quoted as saying.

In the three and a half years since the article, Meg and Piper had remained in touch. And, in that time, Piper and Richard fell in love.

Piper wanted similar happiness for Meg — who was not, she told Piper, the falling-in-love type.

That was fine, Piper replied. She had a friend, a trauma surgeon who'd briefly dated a roommate of hers, who felt exactly the same way.

They should meet, Piper said. They'd like each other. They certainly *were* alike, she noted, based on their mutual refusal to be introduced to the other.

Meg had no interest in a gorgeous, gifted surgeon. He'd be arrogance personified. With good reason, perhaps. But no, thank you. A further truth, which she didn't share, was that she'd given up dating years ago.

Mark had no interest in a gorgeous, gifted pillowmaker — who, as far as Piper knew, still maintained her two-month dating rule. True, he avoided long-term relationships. But the pillow woman's rule was shallow. Insulting.

Too much like looking in the mirror? he wondered privately.

Mark Traynor had known that Meg Gallagher would be at the engagement party hosted by the Murrays for their son and his bride. He'd expected to see Meg, to spot her from a distance and steer clear. She'd be in the middle of the room, the center of attention, surrounded by a wall of admirers three or four men thick.

But the only woman who matched Piper's description — tall, striking, blond, single — stood in a shadowed corner, leaning against a window, positioned as if that was where she intended to stay until she could take her leave.

The man who'd planned to avoid her like

the plague crossed decisively toward her.

"You must be Meg." He'd invaded her shadows, he realized, as she started, stiffening at his soft but intruding voice.

Her turn toward him was graceful and yet reluctant.

Tired, too.

Her expression matched the weary pirouette.

Then, before his eyes, she transformed herself as dramatically as her pillows transformed tired-looking houses. He watched it happen, the summoning of energy, the gearing up for the game.

The finding of dazzle deep inside.

"I must be?"

"Yes."

"And you are?"

"Mark." That should've been all he needed to say. He knew for a fact that Piper's mission to introduce them had been pursued as aggressively with Meg as with him. "Traynor. You've heard of me."

Of course she had. Trauma surgeon. Ice in his veins. Her frown suggested she had only the vaguest memory. "You're a surgeon or something."

Mark smiled. "Where's your man of the month?"

Her eyes widened, as if she didn't have a

clue what he was talking about. "I'm here alone. And your woman of the night?"

"Ouch. I'm alone tonight. Too." To meet her, after all? If so, his subconscious had been keeping it secret. "I'm intrigued by your two-month rule."

Meg sighed. "Piper should really stop telling people about that."

"Because it no longer applies?"

"Because it sounds so . . ."

Obnoxious, Mark would have said, and had said to Piper. But *obnoxious* didn't seem so appropriate now. "Arbitrary?"

"Silly."

"But it's still in effect?"

"Sure!"

"And if, at the end of two months, you'd like to continue seeing him?"

"It's never happened."

"And if he wants to continue seeing you?"

"He'll get over it."

"You're that forgettable?"

"Let's talk about you."

"Be my guest. I'm an open book." And you, Meg Gallagher, are not. Even her two-month rule had a hidden reason for being. It wasn't about men, or how boring, in her experience, they became. The devaluation wasn't of her dates, but of herself. Forgettable Meg — her words. Memorable Meg

. . . his. Women he'd known wanted more than two months, and a lot more than sex. Meg really didn't. "You're a seamstress."

"I make pillows."

"Your pillows don't have seams?"

"A few seams. Very easy. I thought we were talking about you."

"We are. We're talking about things I'd like to know — about you. You enjoy making pillows, and decorating homes for sale."

"I do. Very much. Thinking of turning in your scalpel and finding a new line of work?"

"I'm where I'm supposed to be. I gather you are, too."

"Yes. I am. See how different we are? I'm happy with fluff, you're dedicated to meaning."

"You save houses," Mark countered. "Sometimes, if fate's with me, I'm able to make an impact on lives."

"They're *not* equivalent."

"In the greater scheme of things? How do you know?" She wasn't going to answer that, he decided. And she believed — incorrectly — that he was mocking her. "You've had other jobs."

"A few," Meg replied. "I was a neurosurgeon for a while."

Mark smiled. "Not your cup of tea?"

"Not my cup of tea."

"Neurosurgery aside, did you enjoy any of your previous endeavors?"

"Neurosurgery aside, I enjoyed all of them."

"But not forever."

"I imagine Piper's told you I used to change jobs about as often as I change men."

"She has told me that. She said you drove for UPS?"

"One of my first jobs."

"What did you like about it?"

"You really want to know this?"

"I really do."

"Okay. Well. The uniform was nice. Not the *color* necessarily, but the fact of a uniform. No quandaries about what to wear. More time, in the morning, to stay in bed."

If her allusion to bed was meant to be provocative, Mark thought, it failed. It came off as tired, not seductive. She wasn't trying to seduce him, of course. Quite the opposite. The bed comment had been dutiful. Something the dazzling Meg would be expected to say.

She'd failed on all counts. She didn't want to seduce him.

But she was.

"The uniform's a perk," he said, "of being a surgeon, too. Scrubs and coats. Very easy. More sleep. What else did you like about UPS?"

"The exercise."

"And?"

"Leaving the sorting facility with a truck full of packages and returning with an empty one."

"Sense of accomplishment."

"Let me guess," Meg said. "It's just like performing lifesaving surgery every day."

She smiled a little as she awaited his reply. Her smile was faint, Mark noted, but true. "I hate to tell you this, Meg, but it's actually pretty similar."

"No, it's not!"

"Yes, it is. I made it through my internship by crossing one item after another off my scut list. I'm still a surgeon. You left UPS. Why?"

"Time to move on."

It was the truth, he decided. But not the *whole* truth. "You can do better than that."

"Okay, then. Fumes."

And that was a complete lie.

An anxious one. She looked uncomfortable, as if those fumes were making it hard for her to breathe . . . making her eager to flee. She didn't have the energy to spar with him, and the alternative, letting down her guard, was even worse, Mark decided.

She was going to flee. But, he realized, she hated to leave the shadows at the edge of the party — for fear, perhaps, of being thrust into its center.

Mark wasn't the kind of man to force himself on anyone who didn't want his company. He was hard pressed to remember the last time the message to stay away had been this clear. Hard pressed to remember such a message — ever.

But when it was a matter of her wishes versus his, there wasn't any contest.

"Nice meeting you, Meg."

Her surprise at his words became a mixture of gratitude and relief. "It was nice meeting you, too, Mark."

He left her, in the shadows, where she wanted to be . . . and where, he guessed, she was taking deep, grateful breaths that he was gone.

She was relieved.

And he was lost.

He wandered far from her shadows, and even engaged in light banter with other party guests.

But his thoughts were with her.

He wanted to take her to bed. That was a given. The attraction — for him — had been immediate and strong. He wanted to make love to Meg, and more. A nakedness that had nothing to do with sex.

Maybe in bed, she'd let him know the real Meg, the true Meg . . . and why that Meg — the memorable one — believed she was forgettable.

Mark wandered. His thoughts wandered.

He finally calmed the restlessness with a plan.

He'd say goodbye. And, if she greeted his new farewell as gratefully as she'd greeted his previous one, that would be that.

"Me again," he said when he reached her.

"Mark. Hi."

"Hi," he echoed to eyes that seemed more relieved by his return than his departure . . . as if she'd been lost, wandering restlessly, too.

"I wanted to tell you something."

"And I want to ask you something. Ladies first."

"It's about my reason for leaving UPS."

"Not fumes."

"Not fumes. I had the same route every day. It was a good route. It took me to a part of Seattle I'd never been to. I got to know some of my regular customers. Not well, but in a generally positive context. I delivered packages they were delighted to receive. There was one woman in particular, a stay-at-home mom with three lively children of her own and assorted dogs and neighbor kids visiting virtually every time I made a delivery."

"A happy scene."

"Very happy. And there was excitement in her future. A second honeymoon — a cruise — while her parents babysat the kids. It was autumn in Seattle. She ordered tropical outfits from stores on-line, and a few evening gowns, too. She showed me some of them. Opened the boxes the minute I delivered them to her. I'm making this too long a story."

"Not for me."

"Well. Needless to say she was in a good mood whenever I saw her. Until the day she answered the door in tears. Her children, inside without their friends, had been crying, too. She wouldn't be needing the package I was delivering that day. Or any of the packages. There'd be no second honeymoon. Her husband was having an affair, moving out, filing for divorce."

"That's too bad," he murmured.

"Yes."

"And?"

"Oh. And, that afternoon, I gave my notice."

"Okay," Mark said quietly. "Why?"

"You know what they say, don't you? When the emotions get tough . . ."

"When the emotions get tough," he repeated.

"The not-so-tough get going. Pretty feeble, isn't it? Pretty . . . cowardly."

"Surely there were friends."

"I don't understand."

"Friends, other than you, that the woman whose marriage had broken up could talk to."

"Oh." Meg frowned. "I mean, yes, there were. She had lots of friends."

"Now I'm the one who doesn't understand. You quit your job at UPS because you didn't want to help a woman you barely knew deal with a tough emotional time. Yes?"

"No. If she'd needed my help, I'd have helped. The emotions I didn't want to deal with were mine."

"Ah," he said softly. "Her sadness made you sad."

"And mad. So I went away. As I said, pretty feeble. Pretty cowardly."

"Pretty honest, I'd say." And fragile. And lovely. "Are you ready for my question?"

She seemed surprised he still planned to ask it. "Yes."

"How do I sign up?"

"To drive for UPS?"

"To spend two months with you."

Meg opened her eyes, aching with remembrance, in need of champagne.

She looked from the falling snow to the glass in her hand.

It was full. Brimming. And the level in the bottle was unchanged from when she'd set it beside her on the floor.

She hadn't been drinking.

No wonder she hurt so much.

She needed to drink, quickly, now.

She didn't. She looked up instead, to the falling snow, and noticed a blinking reflection on the window pane — an answering machine message she hadn't checked.

One message, the single blink told her, that had been received, the electronic voice announced, hours ago.

Caroline. Saying cheerful things, expected things — and unexpected ones. She'd found out about the stuffed animals, and approved — with a fondness that made Meg hurt all over again.

She hurt even more, so much more, when Caroline spoke of the petticoat sky — as if Caroline longed, as she did, for the girls who'd searched the heavens for lace. And snow . . .

What innocents they'd been, Meg at four, Caroline at eight. And innocent still, although their world was shattered two years later, when Caroline followed the sound of ice cubes to her.

Meg had seen Caroline's fear as she'd commanded Meg to stop.

And her alarm, and her confusion, when Meg's response was to take bigger gulps. To drink faster.

And Caroline's fierceness when she reached for the glass and pulled it away.

She'd been so mad at Caroline.

But there'd been other feelings, remembered later. Gratitude that Caroline cared, and kept caring, even when Meg defied her command. And wanting to surrender to Caroline, to be held by Caroline, even as she was resisting Caroline's attempts to help.

Meg wanted to drink. Now. Surrender now.

There was no one here to stop her, or hold her.

No one but herself.

What I'm wondering, Meg, is whether you've ever considered giving up alcohol for you . . .

Okay, so Mark was here. In spirit.

And Caroline, too. And Jeffrey. And the baby Meg would carry for them.

It was that houseful of spirits, she told herself, that encouraged her to pour the champagne — every untouched bottle — slowly but surely down the drain.

CHAPTER EIGHT

Monday, February 14

On the day before jury selection began, Meg and Caroline kept appointments at the Reproductive Medicine Clinic at QAMC. Neither knew the other would be there, and Meg arrived twenty minutes after Caroline left.

For both, the news was good.

Caroline passed her one-month exam with flying colors.

And, once a few of her questionnaire answers had been explained to the satisfaction of the clinic psychologist, Meg underwent an entirely normal physical exam.

Not surprisingly, the psychologist's additional inquiries had been about her drinking. Meg had checked yes, for example, in response to "Have you ever consumed in excess of two drinks a day, every day, for a month?" That had tripped a search for more specific information. How many drinks per day? How many days, months, years in a row?

The psychologist knew, from the questionnaire, the last time Meg had anything to drink. She didn't know if there'd been symptoms of withdrawal. No, Meg had assured her. None.

And how had Meg been doing since?

Quite well . . . really. Lots of energy. Lots of exercise to match. Keeping busy with her work.

There'd been a series of written questions about domestic violence. Do you feel safe where you live? Have you ever been physically threatened? Or struck? Is there somewhere you can go if you feel you're in danger? Would you like information about such places?

None of the questions applied to her. But she'd felt sadness, and anger, for the women — and babies — for whom they did. Her replies, on the questionnaire, had all been "No."

The psychologist reconfirmed them verbally, nonetheless.

The physician who examined Meg did a little reconfirming, too. The last time she'd had intercourse was nine months ago? On April 13th? And she'd had the same sexual partner for the three months leading up to and including that date? And, before that partner, she'd had no sexual intercourse — no sexual *anything* — for seven years?

By the time Meg left the clinic, all that remained in her surrogacy eligibility process were the results of the lab tests taken after her exam. They'd be available when she returned for her followup appointment in three and a half weeks.

If the results were good, Meg thought as she departed the medical center without veering toward a certain terrace, a certain man, she'd present her case to Caroline. She'd been thinking about her sister non-stop . . . but, during the past month of sobriety and waiting, she'd spoken to her only twice.

That evening, while Meg exercised away excess energy before starting to sew, Caroline wrote in her journal before the nap from which she planned to awaken when Jeffrey got home.

Happy Valentine's Day!
You're a month old, and doing gloriously. Would you like to hear your progress to date? I have, of course, been reading about it.
You have a "primitive" face, with dark circles

for eyes and the earliest beginnings of a mouth and jaw.

I knew about your mouth. How else could you be my constant smile?

I hadn't realized, before my reading, how big you'd be today — or rather how small.

One-quarter inch. That's it. That's all. That's everything.

That's you.

The books describe a quarter of an inch as smaller than a grain of rice. I'd describe it as quite a bit smaller. I know measurements, you see.

As an architect, I use 1/4" — for scale — all the time.

Most of the time, 1/4" represents a foot. When I'm designing something truly grand, it can represent a yard or two or ten.

Until now, I'd have considered myself an authority on things a quarter of an inch long.

But I'm not an authority at all.

Until now, I had no idea how grand its scale could be.

I had no idea, until you, that one-quarter inch is the size of a dream.

CHAPTER NINE

Meg had known since Thursday. But she'd had to wait until today, when Judge Owens's courtroom would be dark, to have a reasonable chance of seeing Jeffrey.

Jury selection was going well, the newspapers reported. It might even be completed by Friday — in which case opening statements would be a week from tomorrow.

That would give Caroline and Jeffrey an eight-day window to consider her offer before the trial began.

If their answer was yes, she, Caroline and Dr. Collier could move forward with the process while Jeffrey took care of Kevin Beale.

If their answer was yes.

Meg had never been to Jeffrey's office. But

she had no trouble finding it.

"I'm Meg Gallagher," she explained to the attractive woman who smiled as she entered. "Jeffrey's sister-in-law."

"And I'm Sheila Eitner. His administrative assistant. What can I do for you?"

"I don't have an appointment. But I was hoping Jeffrey might have a few minutes to see me this afternoon. If not . . ."

Sheila waved away Meg's concern. "He has time. Although, at the moment, he's with Susannah's family at their hotel. I expect him back within the hour, but it could be longer. I'm reluctant to page him."

"And I don't want you to. I'm happy to wait."

Dearest whirling dervish,
You've really got me spinning, with a little wooziness mixed in.

"We often see this," Kathleen tells me. "Hormones."

I don't mind! I love any and all proof that you're making yourself at home inside me.

I'm so thrilled you've decided to stay. You're happy, too, aren't you? Every day, and ever more brightly, I feel your smile.

Your dad and I were talking about you last night. We talk about you all the time. Already you're our life.

I want to share a special part of last night's conversation with you.

We were recalling the pledge we'd made to live every day of our marriage as if it was our wedding day (without the chaos), to remember our love every day as we go through life hand in hand.

That sounds easy, doesn't it? And, I would guess, far from unique. What newlyweds wouldn't make such promises?

We love each other even more today than on our wedding day. But despite our best intentions, there've been times when our busy lives have gotten us off track . . . pulled our hands apart . . . made us forget our pledge.

Your dad's dedicated to keeping criminals as far away from pregnant moms and beloved children as the law allows. As a result, he gets completely involved in the cases he's prosecuting. That's why he's so terrific at what he does. It's important work — more so now that you're on the way.

My work, of course, *isn't* life and death. But it's life, designing homes for families, happy places for love. I get involved in my projects, too, as distracted by the myriad minor problems at a job site as he gets distracted by evidence that wasn't collected quite as impeccably as the defense attorneys will insist it should have been.

I get tense. He gets tense. We've even been known to snarl . . . and quarrel. But you know how such rocky episodes always end? Don't worry! I'm keeping my promise not to share intimate details you haven't the slightest wish to hear. One of us inevitably tumbles to the obvious — that it's the stress of our jobs, not fissures in our love, that's wreaking havoc.

We're so on track at the moment I honestly don't believe we'll ever let ourselves derail again. How could we, when you're here, too, and it's the three of us now, hand in hand *in hand.*

We made a new pledge last night, a pledge to you. We're going to do everything in our power to make each and every day of your life as happy as it can be. That sounds easy, too, doesn't it? We want that for you, more than anything, happiness upon happiness.

It all seems possible on this rainy, cozy, whirling day. *Everything* seems possible. It's as if someone — we both know who — has given me rose-colored glasses.

Interestingly enough, my designs have a reputation for being cozy — my Seattle designs, that is. Before moving here, I specialized in sleek office buildings, not single-family homes.

But that's what I wanted to design here — and, thank heavens, my partners agreed.

I *can* do sleek in private homes. But every architect has a favorite style, and mine, I've discovered, is colonial.

As I'm writing this, I'm wondering why. I've assumed it was simply an aesthetic appreciation.

But now I'm sensing there's something else, something more — as if, once upon a time, your mom had rose-colored glasses of her own.

Give me a minute, little one. I'm going to see if what I'm sensing can become more clear . . .

. . . it's been many minutes, but what a discovery I've made!

In the eighteen years since the incident with Meg, I haven't spent much time searching for happy memories before that day.

Why would I? Meg's revelation that she'd always hated me provided a pretty vivid assessment of our girlhood years.

But now I've glimpsed an earlier image. A happy one.

Meg and I are cuddled together in bed, in the rambler on Cherry Circle Drive, peering at a book as I read aloud.

Meg's three, a bright-eyed cherub with golden ringlets, mesmerized by the words — " 'Twas the night before Christmas." She's also entranced, as I am, by the drawing of the place where visions of sugar plums dance in dreams and stockings are hung by the chimney with care and Santa lands on the rooftop amid hooved clatter and chiming sleigh bells.

On that long-ago night, Meg and I snuggled in that storybook house.

Storybook colonial.

Do you suppose she remembers?

Yes, you're right. I could ask her.

But asking Meg if she happens to recall the happy Christmas memory might precipitate a deafening silence — and undo in one fell swoop the progress we've managed to achieve. Progress in moving away from the past . . .

Not that I'm not tempted to ask her. I am.

So how's this for a plan? We do an on-line search — bookstores, eBay, libraries — for the identical picture book Meg and I had as girls. It would've been published thirty years ago, and would have been inexpensive at the time, and who knows how many versions of the classic poem have been published since?

But there's a copy of *our* version somewhere.

And we'll find it.

Then, when we invite Aunt Meg over to celebrate your first Christmas Eve, I'll read aloud to you from the copy we've found.

Or your dad will.
Or, just maybe, Aunt Meg will.

CHAPTER TEN

King County Prosecutors' Office
Monday, March 14
3:45 p.m.

Jeffrey's expression held concern before he spotted Meg. His thoughts, as he entered his office, were with the grieving family with whom he'd spent the better part of the afternoon.

That concern didn't vanish when he noticed his sister-in-law. It merely shifted, and deepened.

"Meg?"

"Nothing's happened to Caroline," she reassured him as she stood up. "I was just hoping you'd have a moment to spare."

"Of course. Please come in." When they were in his office behind closed doors, he asked, "Are you all right?"

"Perfectly. So much so that I'm here to offer my services in the baby department."

"Your . . . services?"

"As an incubator. Genetically, the baby would be Caroline's and yours. That's been the difficulty, hasn't it? The in vitro part takes, but the in vivo — I've learned all the terms — is problematic. I thought if you and Caroline did the in vitro, and I did the in vivo, maybe there'd be a baby — Why are you looking at me like that?"

At that precise moment Jeffrey was thinking how much her expression resembled Caroline's when she talked about Meg. A blend of uncertainty . . . and hope. He hadn't seen it before on Meg, and had always felt ambivalence — tending toward dislike — about his sister-in-law. How dare she cause the woman he loved such sadness? But now . . . "It's a very generous offer."

"Not really. It's just something I can do, would *like* to do —"

"Meg? Really. It is."

Meg shrugged, and focused on his frown. "Generous or not, I guess Caroline wouldn't go for it."

"I'm sure she would."

"But there's a *but.*"

"She's pregnant."

"Oh, Jeffrey. I didn't know. I haven't spoken to Caroline for a while. Not that she'd have told —"

"We haven't told anyone, Meg. We decided to wait until we were safely through the first trimester."

"How soon will that be?"

"The baby's sixty-one days today."

Meg suspected he could've told her the minutes. And seconds. Caroline could have, too. "Sixty-one days. That's *great.*"

"Yes," Jeffrey said softly. "It is. We're very hopeful. Caroline's feeling all sorts of hormonal effects, and everything that can be measured is exactly where it's supposed to be."

"Then I won't take any more of your time. As busy as this pretrial period has been, it'll probably feel like a vacation once the trial begins. Whatever remaining free moments you have, you'll want to spend with Caroline."

"All that's true — but not so fast. You came to see me, not Caroline. Why?"

"I was planning to make my pitch to Caroline. But as I got to thinking about it, I decided it would be easier to run it by you. I'd be able to deliver my entire spiel without getting sidetracked."

"Your entire spiel."

"Yes, well, I was going to assure you that I've been thoroughly vetted by the surrogacy experts at QAMC. I've taken, and passed, all the prepregnancy exams. I'm in good health and I'm ready, willing and able to follow Kathleen Collier's instructions to the letter. The right food, no alcohol, plenty of rest, no men. Anything a responsible incubator should do, I would do." Meg needed a breath, but didn't pause. "There you have it. My entire spiel. Now can I go?"

"Am I making you that nervous?"

"Yes. Because I know what you're going to say. You want to tell Caroline, don't you?"

"I have to tell her, Meg."

"No, Jeffrey. You don't."

"It's the only way I can explain how I happened to mention her pregnancy to you."

"A perfect example of something else you don't have to tell her."

"But I do."

"Couples *can* keep secrets from each other."

There'd been that one secret. Caroline's decision to try to become pregnant one last time. There'd been a promise, too, made sixty-one nights ago. No more secrets, even good ones — ever.

"Not this secret."

"But it might upset her at a time she shouldn't be upset."

"It won't upset her. In fact, she'll be

delighted that you know about her pregnancy. She needs to know about your offer, Meg. She really does. I can tell her. Or you can. Those are your choices."

"Then you tell her, Jeffrey."

CHAPTER ELEVEN

Monday, March 14
8:45 p.m.
Sweet pea,

Your dad's going to be later than usual, so it'll be a while before he arrives home to share with us whatever mysterious thing he wants to share.

It's something good. That much we know.

Yet more good news on a day already filled with happy tidings.

Today's visit with Kathleen was quite wonderful. You're doing *so well.*

And so am I.

But I'll be thirty-seven by the time you're born.

That's young, by the way, from my perspective — and a twenty-first-century one. From an evolutionary standpoint, however, a thirty-seven-year-old mom is old.

Old*ish,* at any rate. Females of the species

remain most fertile now as they have for millennia: in their teens.

Twenty-first-century doctors are pretty adamant about doing amniocentesis on moms my age.

I don't want the amnio. It's unimaginable that any result could make us decide to — I'm not going to finish that thought. This is my (our) journal. We make the rules. Thoughts needn't be followed to their impossible conclusions if we choose for them not to be.

The test is part of Kathleen's protocol; something I agreed to. I've considered telling her I've changed my mind, exercising my prerogative as a woman, and a hormonally charged one at that. The test can't be performed, after all, without my consent.

"Considered" is an understatement. I've been mulling, worrying, obsessing, nightmaring, what *if* ing about it for weeks. Maybe that's why I'm finally writing about it. I've always believed that if you imagine the worst, it won't happen.

The worst *isn't* going to happen when it comes to the amnio. The best is. You'll be fine, DNA-wise, plus we'll have the fun of knowing whether you're a boy or a girl.

We don't care! We've never cared.

You're the *you* we want.

Keeping my promise is an excellent reason

for having the amnio. But you know the real reason I'm having it?

Your dad.

He wants to believe all is well, and that his heart — our hearts — won't be broken again. We wouldn't make the impossible choice. Period.

Assuming, Caroline thought, their baby was destined to live. She knew all about genetic errors that could preclude an infant from taking even a single independent breath. The downside of reading everything in sight.

After an aching moment, she resumed.

He tries to believe no such sadness is lurking, and he's gallantly hiding his fear. But the fear's there, preventing him from savoring this happy time as fully as he should.

He doesn't have the luxury of feeling your smile. Or the confidence it gives me.

I tell him about it. But he needs more than words.

So we're having the test. For him. So his joy can be as pure as mine.

Okay?

Okay.

Now, my two-month-old, shall I tell you about your growth and development in the past thirty days?

It's extraordinary. You're extraordinary. How much you've accomplished in so little time, all while making your mommy whirl!

Your facial features continue to develop, and your ears are delicate folds of skin. Tiny buds have appeared on your torso, precursors to your arms and legs, with even tinier buds for your fingers and toes.

Your nervous system and digestive tract are coming "on-line," and already cartilage is being replaced by bone.

You're a fetus, the books tell me.

Ha! You're our *baby.*

You're an inch long, having quadrupled in size, and you weigh a third of an ounce.

No wonder I float with you inside me.

A third of your beloved little body is head, and your heartbeat is detectable (by a doctor).

But that's old news, isn't it, as far as we're concerned?

I detected your heart, felt it smiling, sixty-one days ago.

Chapter Twelve

Monday, March 14
9:15 p.m.

Caroline *would* call.

That was who she was. Reliable. Responsible. She always did the right thing, the gracious thing, whether invited to or not.

She'd call, this evening, with an effusive thank-you.

No matter what her true feelings were.

No matter whether she would rather have died than permit a baby of hers to spend nine months inside the sister who'd been so cruel to her on a long-ago April day.

How Caroline would have responded to Meg's offer was moot. She was pregnant. She could pretend to be grateful even if secretly horrified at Meg's presumption in imagining she'd ever have said yes.

The trouble was, Meg had assumed Caroline *would* say yes, that she wouldn't be offended, that she'd trust Meg to keep her baby safe.

But as the minutes passed and the phone didn't ring, Meg made herself examine the data on which she'd based her belief in Caroline's trust.

What data? There wasn't any.

There were merely impressions.

Merely hope.

And the impressions were obviously so off the mark that Caroline was having difficulty forcing sufficient cheer into her voice to make the call.

The pain of that realization prompted another.

Caroline's pregnancy meant that she, Meg, could start drinking again. She was surprised it hadn't occurred to her sooner.

Like the moment she'd left Jeffrey's office.

She could've stocked up on champagne and spent the evening toasting Caroline, Jeffrey and her own newfound freedom.

She had her life back. She could do, could drink, as she pleased.

The more she thought about the sister who hadn't called, the more she needed to drink.

She was thirsty. Her heart was thirsty.

Alcohol's good for some hearts, Mark had conceded. But, he'd implied, not yours.

"Mark Traynor," she said to her silent home. "Another good reason to start drinking."

Or not to.

The contrary thought coincided with the ringing phone.

"Hello?" Her voice was as precarious as she felt.

"Hi, Meg? It's Caroline. Is this an okay time to call?"

"Sure."

"Good. I figured it's been awhile since we talked."

She doesn't know. Jeffrey hasn't told her. "It's been ages. How are you?"

"I'm fine. You?"

"I'm fine, too."

"Busy?"

"Pretty busy. The housing market just keeps booming. As you know." Meg's next logical question would've been to ask how busy her architect sister was. But she'd learned, before leaving Jeffrey's office, that Caroline was putting finishing touches on existing projects and declining new ones. Work questions might be awkward for Caroline. She and Jeffrey had agreed to tell no one about her pregnancy for another month. "Jury selection's going well, or so the reports say."

"The reports are correct. In fact, that — the trial — is one of the reasons I'm calling. I have a question, an invitation of sorts. Feel free to say no, and I don't need an answer before Friday."

"Okay."

"So . . . Do you have any interest in being in the courtroom for opening statements?"

"Are you going to be?"

"Yes. But it's not as hokey as it sounds. My role — our role, if you're game — isn't to be a cheering section for Jeffrey. We'd be his eyes while he's delivering the opening. He'll be watching the jury then, and no one else. We'd watch the jury, too, to gauge their reaction, but also the defense and the gallery."

"Have you done this before?"

"A few times, in Denver, when Jeffrey felt it might be useful. It's fine if you don't want to, Meg. Perfectly fine."

Meg did want to — once she knew Caroline still wanted her to go. "Opening statements will be a week from tomorrow?"

"Probably. They definitely won't be earlier. But could be a day or two later. If so, Jeffrey wouldn't need your answer until the morning before."

"He has to get me a pass?"

"Yes. The first two rows are reserved for

family and witnesses for the respective sides. During the opening, seating in those rows will be assigned. Before Jeffrey begins his statement, Judge Owens will identify everyone who's seated there."

"Is that usual?"

"No. Nothing's usual about this case. That's why it makes sense for the jury to know who's who. They've been hearing rumors about Susannah's family and friends — and Kevin's family and friends — for months. Introducing them means the jury won't become distracted, trying to guess. Judge Owens is also going to admonish the jurors not to draw conclusions based on who's present or absent on any given day. Potential witnesses have to excuse themselves when testimony's presented that might overlap with theirs. And, for family especially, there may be testimony that's too difficult to hear. In essence, she's going to ask the jury to meet everyone during opening statements, and ignore them thereafter."

"Will you be there often?"

"In court? I don't think so. I'll do most of my watching on TV. But the judge wants to introduce me — and you — just in case. She'll give names and relationships. I'll be introduced as Jeffrey's wife. You'd be his sister-in-law."

"Would we have to have noncommittal expressions on our faces during the introductions?"

"I'm afraid so."

Meg heard her sister's laugh. She loved hearing it, and knowing she was its cause. "Even though we believe beyond the shadow of a doubt that Kevin Beale is guilty as sin?"

The accused was presumed innocent in the eyes of the law. And he was being treated that way. But Meg and Caroline were entitled to their opinions. Caroline's opinion was, of course, an informed one. Caroline couldn't reveal specifics of what Jeffrey had told her. But her certainty that Kevin Beale had committed cold-blooded murder was enough for Meg.

"Even though," Caroline affirmed.

"I really hate that I made pillows for the houseboat."

"You had no idea he'd be buying it, Meg. Or, for that matter, who he was."

"True, and true. I also hate how much I enjoyed making the pillows, and being there. It was so charming. Romantic. Private. The ideal venue for a sociopath to commit murder by drowning — without a witness in sight. I can't wait until Kevin Beale is where he belongs."

"Let's just hope it happens."

"Do you doubt it, Caroline?"

"I don't doubt his guilt, or Jeffrey's ability to present the case exactly as it needs to be. But no matter how impartial a jury says it can be, and Jeffrey's very happy with the jurors selected so far, Kevin's celebrity — and popularity — can't be discounted. People feel they know him. And they *like* him. It's hard to imagine anyone doing what he did, much less someone they'd happily invite into their homes. Accepting his guilt also tells them how faulty their instincts are. They want to believe they would've been able to spot a sociopath in their midst."

"You really think he could be found not guilty?"

"Oh, yes."

"Does Susannah's family know?"

"That there might be an acquittal? Yes. Well, Jeffrey's told them. Whether they've truly comprehended that the man who murdered their daughter and grandson could go free is another matter."

"He won't go free. Jeffrey will get him."

"He'll do his best. He's got an excellent team."

"He'll do it, Caroline."

"I hope — *oh.*"

"Caroline? What's wrong?"

"I heard a noise," she whispered. "I think

someone's in the house."

"*Stay where you are.* I'll use my cell phone to call 911."

"Okay. No — wait! Jeffrey? . . . It's him, Meg. Sorry for the alarm. I didn't expect him home for hours. He did say he had good news, though. Maybe Kevin's done something incredibly decent, like admitting his guilt. Wouldn't *that* be lovely?"

"Very. Well, you'd better go."

"Okay. And about being in court . . . it's fine, Meg, whatever you want to do."

CHAPTER THIRTEEN

A confession from the murderer *would* be lovely.

And Meg's willingness to carry her sister's baby? Would Caroline regard that as lovely, too?

Meg would have her answer soon.

It wouldn't take Jeffrey long to share the news. And, knowing Meg was waiting, Caroline would offer her a gracious — if false — thank-you, without having the opportunity to rehearse.

Even if Caroline's gratitude was authentic, the call was bound to be awkward.

When the emotions get tough, the not-so-tough get going . . . or get drinking . . . or, in the case of Margaret Elizabeth Gallagher, both.

She was free, *free,* to do both right now.

She could grab her parka, jog to the nearby store and pick up where she'd left off on a snowy night two months ago.

Before listening to the answering-machine message Caroline would leave, she could be drenched in the numbness she'd given up — for Caroline — and had no reason to deprive herself of any longer.

No reason whatsoever.

So why wasn't she reaching for her parka and dashing out the door?

Something was stopping her. The same thing, perhaps, that had stopped her whenever she'd wanted to drink since January.

You hurt? Too bad! This is for Caroline, remember? Just say no.

She'd said no for the past two months. It had been difficult, and yet so easy, to do.

More difficult would be saying no for herself. That would require getting over the aching that yearned for numbness. Or getting through it. She'd have to run toward the tough emotions, not away.

There was a middle ground when it came to the suddenly ringing phone.

Meg neither moved toward it, nor away.

The message was recorded in silence.

Only when the message light blinked did she walk over to the machine and listen to her sister's call.

"You're not there, I guess. Or on the phone. Probably just as well. My emotions are pretty shaky as it is. Jeffrey just told me,

Meg. I'm overwhelmed. And grateful. And humbled and honored — and weepy. As you can hear. Very weepy. And getting worse. Damn! I was afraid this would happen . . . I'm trying a few deep breaths . . . still trying . . . *okay.*

"I'm thrilled you know about the baby. I've wanted to tell you. But, as Jeffrey explained to you, we'd agreed to wait. I almost told you anyway, tonight, when you were saying how much you hated having made pillows for Kevin Beale's houseboat. I was going to ask you if you'd be willing to make a pillow or two for a baby I'm beginning to know? And who's going to love knowing his or her Aunt Meg?

"I've already been raving about you to your niece or nephew. Raving in writing. I'm keeping a journal. Have you ever done that? I never had. I'm finding it a very interesting — and very *revealing* — thing to do. I'm making discoveries about myself. Like how soft and emotional I can be — and how good such emotions feel.

"I'll become physically soft, too, as the pregnancy progresses. Not to mention huge . . . but so what, as long as it *does* progress . . . forgive my shaky sigh . . . and keep your fingers crossed, please . . . and thank you again, Meg, *so* much. The way it makes me feel to know you would've carried my baby for me . . . well, I wish I could transfer that soaring feeling to you."

Caroline's goodbye was a weepy jumble of thank-you and surrender.

Meg surrendered, too, to every aching — soaring — impulse. She reached for the phone and compelled her trembling fingers to dial.

"Caroline?"

"Did you get my message?"

"Yes. Thank you."

"Meg. Thank *you.*"

"You're welcome!"

"It's just so —"

"You're *welcome.* You've thanked me enough."

"I could never thank you enough," Caroline said. "But, if you like, I'll stop doing it."

"Please."

"Okay."

Okay, Meg echoed in silence. Now what? She'd made the call impulsively. Without thinking about the things she might say. The kind of call *sisters* made. "Are you feeling all right?"

"Better than all right. *Pregnant.* My main symptom so far has been the whirlies. This little one's made me pretty dizzy."

"You're not driving."

"Not until the dizziness subsides. Kathleen's predicting that'll be in another week or two."

"How are you getting around in the meantime?"

"I really haven't needed to very much. The beauty of working at home. That plus the electronic transmission of blueprints. For my once-a-month doctor's appointments, I've taken a cab."

"Food?"

"Jeffrey's first trip to the grocery store netted enough food to last forever. And he's made a few trips since."

"But you might suddenly need, I don't know, a different flavor of ice cream and a jar of pickles."

"That hasn't happened yet."

"Clothes?"

"That's going to become an issue one of these days. And I *could* use a personal shopper."

"We'll do it. I'll drive. Then, and *any* time. You know how flexible my schedule is."

And I'll be sober, Meg vowed, day and night. Sober for Caroline.

The aching, soaring impulses that had compelled the phone call weren't finished yet. They took Meg's pledge and ran with it, running toward the tough emotions, not away.

Sober — still — for Caroline.

And sober — at last — for you.

CHAPTER FOURTEEN

King County Courthouse
Tuesday, March 22
10:00 a.m.

Judge Owens made the introductions as well as they could possibly be made. Like a minister presiding over a wedding, she was equally deferential to those seated on both sides of the aisle, the family and friends of the murdered bride — and of the murderous groom.

Jeffrey should've begun his opening statement then.

But Marteen requested a sidebar. It was the legal equivalent of asking for a time-out before a potentially game-winning play. The critical player, his adrenaline already peaking, was put on ice.

Jeffrey wasn't surprised by the tactic, clichéd though it was. Marteen wouldn't let originality get in the way of using every trick in a defense counsel's book.

Whispers filled the courtroom during the sidebar.

And the killer stared at Meg.

He'd looked at her earlier, when she was introduced. He'd looked at everyone on the prosecution side. His expression had been predictable and — undoubtedly — practiced.

A little solemn. A little sad.

The expression hadn't changed during any of the introductions, but it had lingered when it fell on Meg.

The sidebar stare was different. The live feed was blank. The TV stations' legal analysts were making whatever rushed comments the time-out would allow. For the moment, no one was watching him.

It was an insolent stare, and a degrading one. A visual undressing.

Meg returned it with a glower.

"Meg," Caroline whispered.

Meg's glower became a dismissive frown before turning from Kevin to Caroline.

"What a jerk!" Meg whispered, too. "Why's he doing that?"

"Because you're so beautiful."

"I'm not, but even if I were, he finds it amusing to flirt *in court* with the prosecutor's sister-in-law? How pathological can he get?"

"As pathological," Caroline replied, "as a so-called human being can be."

"Good point," Meg murmured as the courtroom hushed.

The sidebar was over.

Jeffrey was ready to begin.

He had to wait a little longer. Marteen was listening to some bit of information his client apparently felt it necessary to impart then and there. The defense counsel seemed acutely aware of how inappropriate this particular on-camera delay might appear.

He whispered something to Kevin. A moment later, Jeffrey had their full attention — and gave his full attention to the citizens who'd determine Kevin Beale's fate.

"Ladies and gentlemen of the jury," he began. "When a murder is committed, it becomes the responsibility of the state to speak for the victim. We — the other members of the prosecutorial team and I — become her voice. We name the killer she's no longer able to name. And, for her, we seek justice. She's helping us in this quest. In her struggle to save herself and her baby, Susannah Nichols left us critical bits of evidence.

"All of you came to this courtroom with impressions about the defendant, and Susannah, and the facts of the case. Mr. Marteen and I discussed this with you during voir dire. Anyone who follows the news has been inundated with information — and misinformation — for the past seven months. That's okay. We want jurors who are in touch with the world. And every one of you has promised to base your verdict solely on testimony and evidence presented to you during the trial.

"We believe you'll keep that promise. We also realize it's easier said than done. The rumors are there, in your consciousness, and it's impossible to unring a bell. To stop knowing what you know — or think you know. I have a promise for you in return. We — the state of Washington speaking on Susannah and Matthew's behalf — will reveal the truth as our witnesses, and the evidence, reveals it to be.

"You may find yourselves thinking that what you're hearing in court isn't even close to what you've previously read. You may wonder if we're withholding key facts, or misrepresenting the relevance of what we do present.

"That's not what we do. Let me say that again. Not what we do. The justice system doesn't ask you to accept my word. And Mr. Marteen won't be reticent to share with you any dispute he has with our case.

"But, and I know I'm repeating myself, you must base your verdict on what you hear, in sworn testimony, in this courtroom. Nothing else."

Jeffrey let a few seconds pass before shifting gears.

"Now," he said. "Speaking of what you'll be hearing, I'd like to tell you what that will be. Before I start, I want to address apprehensions some of you may have about certain evidence you'll be asked to examine. You may be worried about looking at the crime-scene and postmortem photographs. I'd be surprised if you weren't.

"I need you to concentrate on the testimony that's before you, undistracted by what you may or may not be asked to consider in the future. I can tell you today, with certainty, that I won't ever ask you to view postmortem images of baby Matthew. You're the first to know of this decision. The defense is hearing it as you do."

Jeffrey paused, glancing at each juror in turn. "Do I want a guilty verdict? You bet. I believe it's the correct verdict. The just one. And achievable, I believe, based on evidence, not emotion.

"You're all adults. You don't need to see a photograph of an infant who could have lived, and was mature enough at the time of his murder *to* have lived, to know the horrific nature of the crime that stole his life.

"The photographs I will show you — of Susannah — aren't meant to shock you into a guilty verdict, or to anger you into it. That's not the kind of verdict I want you to render. I'll show you the photographs because of the critical evidence they reveal. They're disturbing. Murder *is* disturbing. And it would trouble Susannah to know you're disturbed.

"But that thoughtful woman is dead. And, in the photographs I'll ask you to look at on her behalf, she's pointing the way to her killer."

Jeffrey paused again, for his words to take hold.

"There will be no crime-scene photographs shown today. Not by me. And I'll let you know in advance when I plan to present them. But there *are* photos I'd like you to see today. Snapshots of happier times."

Jeffrey nodded to a colleague at the prosecution table, and, as the slide projector was turned on, he thought about the slides he would show . . . and who had chosen them.

Caroline, in a process that was both lengthy and reverent. Glenn and Dorothy Nichols had responded to his request for photographs with a large box of images of the daughter they'd lost. Caroline had given each treasured memento its due. And when the selections were shown to Glenn and Dorothy, they'd been pleased with the decisions she'd made.

"I'm going to tell you a story," Jeffrey told the jury when the projector was ready. "A true story. I intend to prove its truth to you in the coming weeks. You needn't take notes — unless you want to confirm at some later point that I've delivered on my promises.

"The story begins seventeen months ago, on October 19, during United Airlines flight 566 from Chicago to Seattle. Susannah Nichols was an attendant on that flight. Kevin Beale was a passenger in first class."

Jeffrey pressed a button on the wireless clicker he held in his hand. A color photograph appeared in the nearby screen.

"This is Susannah. Taken by her mother. They'd gone for a walk through the Arboretum earlier that week."

Jeffrey fell silent, letting the photograph tell its own story. Azure sky. Trees adorned in autumnal glory. A woman — a daughter — laughing as her mother insisted on one more shot. The jury had met the mother. They were meeting the daughter now. Her rosy cheeks. Her freckled nose. Her happiness in being with her mother, laughing with her mother, sharing a perfect October day.

"Also taken earlier that week," Jeffrey said as he pressed the button to advance the slide, "is this photograph of the defendant."

The photograph was flattering to the killer.

Jeffrey hadn't needed to select a good picture of Kevin Beale. But he — and Caroline — had. It was a different image of autumn, but an appealing one.

Kevin Beale, reporting from the sidelines, during a game, as the distant scoreboard noted, between the Atlanta Falcons and the Chicago Bears.

"You can see that the defendant's hair was longer when he and Susannah met. It remained about this length until the following July, three weeks before Susannah's death. He had it cut then, on July twenty-fourth, the way you see it now. There's a reason for that haircut and, because it's relevant, I'm going to tell you what it was. The dates are important, too.

"On the day before, Friday the twenty-third, he'd received word that he'd been tapped to do in-the-booth commentary for a major television network. As many of you remember, the rumor that he'd get the job had been circulating since May. In that instance, unlike most other instances in this case, the rumor was true.

"The press conference announcing that he'd been chosen was scheduled for Monday, July twenty-sixth. He arrived wearing what he described to the assembled media as his new 'corporate America' look."

Jeffrey clicked to the next photograph of Susannah. She wore her flight-attendant uniform and the bright eyes and ready smile the jury was beginning to know . . . and needed to know.

"Susannah and the defendant began dating. Dating," Jeffrey repeated. "*Not* falling in love. It was a nice relationship. But, as you'll hear from friends of both Susannah and the defendant, neither expected it, or wanted it, to lead to marriage. Susannah hoped to travel the world. She was scheduled to begin working flights to Europe within the year. The defendant was focused on his broadcasting career.

"Susannah's pregnancy was unplanned. By both of them. Some of you may have come to this courtroom with the understanding that wasn't the case. It's one false rumor I'll be calling witnesses to address.

"Susannah did not — *did not* — try to become pregnant. She wasn't interested in marriage, or in trapping any man — much less a man with whom she didn't expect a future. Don't get me wrong. What if she *had* gotten pregnant on purpose? Would that justify her murder? Of course not. Nothing would. But, on this point, I'll set the record straight.

"Susannah's pregnancy resulted from consensual unprotected intercourse that occurred when the defendant surprised her during a layover in Hawaii. Since she hadn't anticipated seeing him until she returned to Seattle, she hadn't brought any contraception with her. And, although the defendant knew he'd be with Susannah in Hawaii, neither did he. They assumed the risk together."

The next slide, Caroline's choice and one of Dorothy's favorites, showed a slender Susannah wearing jeans. Her pregnancy wasn't visible — except in her radiant smile . . . and the hands that already rested protectively on her lower abdomen.

"Sharing responsibility for the life they'd created was another matter. The defendant ended the relationship the day Susannah told him she was pregnant.

"The defense wants to stipulate that the defendant's initial response to the news of his impending fatherhood was less than positive. That's an understatement, and it's the state's position that you, as the triers of fact, need to hear how *extremely* unhappy about his situation the defendant was.

"The testimony will show that he made repeated attempts to convince — or compel — Susannah to abort their unborn child. His money didn't persuade her. Neither did his pleas, some gentle, most angry.

"You'll also hear testimony about remarks made by the defendant bemoaning what Susannah, by refusing an abortion, was doing to him. In fairness to the defendant, the state will make clear the setting in which the remarks were made. A bachelor party for an old teammate, during which a great deal of alcohol was consumed.

"Susannah's unwillingness to terminate her pregnancy was discussed. The defendant's contempt for the existing law was revealed. Only the woman, he said, has the right to choose. The man has no say at all."

A new image of Susannah filled the screen. Her cheeks glowed, more deeply than in the autumn sun, and she held tight to the now apparent bulge beneath her shirt.

"The defendant expressed his sympathy for Scott Peterson. What choice had Laci given him? Divorce wasn't, in the defendant's opinion, the attractive option it was purported to be. Obviously, Peterson had agreed. The only thing that could truly free him from lifelong responsibility for the wife and baby he didn't want was the remedy he'd chosen — to get rid of the problem once and for all. Peterson's mistake, the defendant insisted, was failing to plan the perfect murder. It would have been 'so easy' — his words, ladies and gentlemen. *So easy.*"

The only sound was the projector advancing one slide forward. Taken indoors, and inelegantly framed, the photograph of Susannah's mother on the telephone provided visual proof that Susannah had inherited her bright eyes from Dorothy. Her laughter, too.

"Susannah's on the other end of the phone," Jeffrey said. "She's calling from the doctor's office, to tell her parents that their first grandchild would be a boy."

Jeffrey looked at the photograph as he explained it. His gaze returned to the jury before continuing.

"The men who'll recount the bachelor-party conversation to you are reluctant witnesses. The defendant's their friend. But these men will testify under oath. The defense will underscore what I've already told you. A great deal of alcohol had been consumed. The state will leave it to your collective experience whether alcohol typically encourages people to say things they don't mean — or things they do."

Marteen didn't leap to his feet. Registering an objection during an opening statement was an etiquette line he was loath to cross. He created a minor commotion, however, as he shifted position in his chair.

Jeffrey paused. Waited. Proceeded only when the defense counsel was still.

"Susannah heard the defendant's aversion to fatherhood loud and clear. She accepted it with a grace beyond her years — and a dignity beyond her finances. She could have sued for child support. It was her legal right to do so. She didn't. Yes, those rumors, too, are false. And some were quite specific, as I recall. Dollar amounts were cited.

"Susannah didn't sue for child support. Or *any* support. She did seek legal representation. She asked her attorney — who, because her parents have granted a waiver of attorney-client confidentiality, will testify before you — to prepare a document releasing the defendant from all responsibility for, and claims to, her unborn child. At her suggestion, the document included an agreement that she'd never tell her son the identity of the man who didn't want him.

"Unfortunately, that didn't guarantee it could remain hidden. After all, the defendant himself had discussed it openly with his friends. But it was the best solution Susannah could offer, and it was far more generous — to the defendant — than what her attorney advised. Even before his new broadcasting contract, the defendant was a wealthy man. The law required him to provide for his child.

"Susannah would provide for her baby. Her parents would help. It would be a modest life, filled with love. The document was signed on June tenth. You'll have the opportunity to review it. Four days later, the defendant closed on the purchase of the houseboat on which he'd made a full-price offer at the end of May.

"It's quite a place," Jeffrey said as he clicked to the first of several shots of the houseboat. "These photos, taken before the murders, were provided by the previous owner. As you can see, it's one of three houseboats on the pier. The farthest from shore, it's also the most private. Access to the pier itself is restricted. It's like any other gated community in that you need a key or a code, or to be buzzed in by a homeowner. The houseboat's small. One bedroom. Ideal for a bachelor. Cramped for a couple. Impractical, for many reasons, for a child.

"But that was okay. The defendant didn't

have a child."

The screen went blank. "That should've been the end of the story. Susannah believed it was. The defendant believed it, too. He voiced his relief to friends. He'd dodged a bullet, he said.

"In retrospect, it was an ill-advised remark. Just like his chilling rant at the bachelor party months before. It's the state's position that in another six weeks, the defendant would find himself planning the kind of 'easy' murder he'd criticized another murderer for failing to do. He would've been more careful about making that remark had he known. As careful as he became once his plan for murder was in the works."

After a moment, Jeffrey looked from the jury to the judge.

"Would this be a good time for a break?" she asked.

"It would, Your Honor."

"All right," Judge Owens said. "The bailiff will escort the jurors to the jury room, and we'll reconvene thirty minutes from now."

CHAPTER FIFTEEN

"Wow," Meg whispered to Caroline.

The judge and jury were gone.

Marteen and his client had also disappeared.

Jeffrey remained in the courtroom. But he wasn't in recess. Members of his team needed to talk to him, and there were people he needed to talk to as well.

And one person, Meg thought, he *wanted* to talk to — but couldn't.

Jeffrey looked at Caroline, though. Meg saw the love in his gaze. She'd seen it before. She guessed his glance held messages only Caroline could read — intimacies Caroline alone could decode.

She guessed right, she decided. Caroline was silent, thoughtful, after Jeffrey necessarily turned his attention to Susannah's family.

Meg was silent, too, for a while after her "wow."

It took Caroline a few beats to respond. "Wow, Meg?"

"Jeffrey's . . . that was . . . *wow*."

"You think it's going well?"

"Caroline." Meg smiled. "What part of *wow* don't you understand? He's terrific, isn't he?"

"Yes. But I'm hardly objective."

"The thing is," Meg said, "I think *I* am. True, it's Jeffrey. My brother-in-law. But it's such a different Jeffrey, and in such a different setting."

"His natural habitat."

"I'd say so. He's not even using notes."

"He never does in openings. Or closings. If you don't know the story of the crime by heart, he says you have no business prosecuting it."

"He certainly knows *this* story. By heart. I really like the way he refers to Susannah as Susannah and you-know-who as the defendant. It makes him an abstraction, not a person. That probably isn't an accident."

"No. But it's working for you?"

"Yes. Although *monster* would be even better. Or psychopath. Or murderer. But that's probably frowned upon in civilized courtrooms. And now you're frowning."

"I'm wondering if you're planning to

watch any of the trial."

"All of it! Recorded if not live. Why?"

"I know it would be very helpful for Jeffrey to get your candid feedback. What's clear, what's unclear, the way a witness came across, questions you wish were asked. Whatever. As if you were a juror."

"I'd be happy to, Caroline, if you really think . . ."

"I really do," Caroline said, standing as Judge Owens entered the courtroom.

It had been precisely thirty minutes.

Time to resume.

Jeffrey continued as though there'd been no break at all.

"So what happened between June tenth, when the defendant signed the papers that enabled him to legally dodge the bullet, and July twenty-fourth, when he got his corporate-look haircut? The answer's as simple as it is repugnant — his career. He'd known he was a candidate for the network job since early May. On June twenty-fifth, the network informed his agent that he was on a short list of three. They'd make their final decision in a month. In the meantime, they were letting the three finalists know there'd be specific expectations of whomever they chose.

"Networks survive on advertising dollars

— revenue from companies who in turn survive on the willingness of the American public to buy their products. Keeping sponsors happy is paramount.

"That wasn't news to either the defendant or his agent. But it was news that came with a warning. An employee who brought unsavory attention to the network was a liability and ran the risk of being fired. *Any* employee, even one as charismatic and articulate as the defendant had demonstrated he could be . . . especially if he'd fathered a child out of wedlock and had no intention of having a long-term relationship with either mother or child. That kind of personal conduct doesn't sit well with sponsors. If the rumor floating around was true, the network representative told Beale's agent, it disqualified him from further consideration.

"You'll hear from network executives about that June twenty-fifth conversation, as well as subsequent ones. They'll also share with you the defendant's sudden and dramatic change of heart. He was going to do the right thing, the 'honorable thing' — his words — after all."

A timeline appeared on the screen. It ran from June twenty-fifth, when the network informed Kevin Beale that certain standards of behavior would be a requirement of the job, through the fifteenth of August, when Susannah's body was found.

"The call between the network and the defendant, in which he pledged to marry the mother of his unborn son and become a paragon of fatherhood — another direct quote — happened here." Jeffrey pointed. "On Monday, June twenty-eighth. Three and a half weeks later, on Friday, July twenty-third, he was told the job was his."

Jeffrey moved his hand from the first date to the second.

"You'll notice I haven't highlighted any dates during those three and a half weeks. The reason is that nothing happened. The defendant made no discernible progress toward making good on what he'd told the network he planned to do. Not that he had to. Until the job was his, he was under no obligation to follow through. And if he didn't get the job, he was under no obligation at all.

"Let me tell you what else the defendant didn't do during this time. You remember how talkative he'd been with friends about the pregnancy he didn't want. Well, he didn't say a word to any of those friends, not *one* word to *any* of them, about marrying Susannah. He kept a low profile during those weeks. We have no way of knowing what he was thinking then. We only know that once he'd been told the job was his, the murder plan was swiftly put in motion.

"He had unwitting accomplices. Carefully selected strangers. Beginning with the barber who cut his hair on the morning of July twenty-fourth. You'll hear from the barber. He'll tell you how honored he was that the defendant trusted him to keep secret the surprise marriage proposal he was planning. The jeweler he met with will tell you the same thing. The defendant didn't look for an engagement ring. He merely arranged to have the store opened early — just for Susannah — on the Sunday morning after he proposed."

Jeffrey moved toward the screen and indicated the mark on the timeline when the Sunday-morning ring selection was to have taken place.

The morning Susannah died.

"The arrangements with the jeweler were made on August second. We believe the defendant knew then that Susannah would be unable to keep the appointment he'd made for August fifteenth. Why didn't he just buy her a ring? We know what he told the jeweler, and what the jeweler will tell you. His future bride, he explained, had confided to him that she loved the Tiffany scene in the movie *Sweet Home Alabama.* He hadn't seen the movie himself, he admitted. But he wanted to create that romantic moment for her."

Caroline had assured him there'd be — women — jurors who'd seen *Sweet Home Alabama* and that, from their reaction when he mentioned it, he'd be able to determine which ones they were. Every female juror had seen the movie, Jeffrey decided. He addressed his next remarks to the two who were seated in the front row of the jury box.

"We've talked to Susannah's friends and family. Not one of them recalls her discussing, much less loving, that scene — or any scene from that particular film. What we do know is that Susannah died before the defendant spent even a penny on an engagement ring for her."

Jeffrey's hand fell away from the screen. "I'm going to ask you to pay attention to the similarity in the testimony of the jeweler and the barber. They'd never met, and provided independent statements about their recollections of what the defendant said. Each described him as excited, almost giddy, when he shared his secret. Each noted, without prompting, that he expressed uncertainty, as if his proposal might be refused. That seemed odd, they each said.

Didn't quite ring true."

Jeffrey returned to the timeline. "On Wednesday, August second, the defendant met with the pastry chef and maître d' at the Yarrow Bay Grill. He wanted a special cake. It had to read 'Will you marry me?' and be presented at his table with great fanfare. The maître d' was responsible for reserving the best table, and for the candle-light and roses, and, if he wouldn't mind, for photographing the moment. With the defendant's blessing, the maître d' could even give copies to the press — assuming, he added, that Susannah's answer to the question written in icing was yes.

"It was all theater, ladies and gentlemen. *All of it.* Performed on a stage of the defen-dant's making, with a cast of characters handpicked by him. They'd corroborate his story in the unlikely event the police wanted corroboration. And, as strangers, they were more credible witnesses than friends would be. They were honest folk, with no reason to lie."

Honest, Jeffrey's expression said. Just like the men and women seated before him. He was confident they'd do their best. His expression said that, too.

"Now," he told them. "I have a question for you. I'll give you the answer after you've spent fifteen seconds or so deciding what your own answer would be. Here goes. No, I apologize. I want to point out one more date on the timeline first. It's here. Monday, August ninth. The day the defendant invited Susannah to have dinner with him the following Saturday. Now the question. How many times between July twenty-third, when the defendant knew the job was his, and August ninth, when he invited her to dinner, do you think he and Susannah spoke? Got that? Okay, let's try another version of my question. Extend the start date to June twenty-eighth, when he had his dramatic change of heart. Now extend back beyond the timeline to April seventh, when Susannah's attorney informed the defendant's attorney that he'd be preparing a document he felt certain the defendant would be delighted to sign. I'll give you a minute. . . ."

It was a full minute legal pundits would subsequently note. A minute, to the second, during which Jeffrey never looked at his watch, or the clock on the courtroom wall.

At the minute's end, he said, "The answers are on the next slide. You'll note, when the slide comes up, that the answers are all the same."

The slide appeared. And read: None.

Jeffrey said nothing. The word spoke for itself.

After what felt like another full minute, but was actually only twenty seconds, a new slide took its place.

Taken in her parents' garden, where she'd lived since quitting work, it showed a very pregnant Susannah. She sat with Dorothy; they were enjoying the sunshine and sipping iced tea. Dorothy looked more like Susannah's sister than her mother, and far too young to be a grandmother. That youthful Dorothy had died when her daughter did. The mother to whom the jury had been introduced had aged dramatically.

Jeffrey gestured toward the slide that had made Caroline so sad she almost hadn't chosen it.

"This was taken an hour before the defendant's August ninth phone call. Susannah had just returned from her eight-month check-up. As I think you can see, and as her doctor will confirm, mom and baby boy were doing well.

"Needless to say, Susannah was surprised by the call. She didn't mind hearing from the defendant, and even welcomed the opportunity to congratulate him on his new job. She'd seen several of the many interviews he'd done since getting the job, and

173

complimented him on how well he'd handled them. Dorothy Nichols heard Susannah's side of that phone call. The defense doesn't want you to hear her testimony. Fought hard to keep it out. But you'll hear what Dorothy had to say. The defendant had been doing a lot of thinking, he said to Susannah, and wanted to talk. In person. Over dinner. When Susannah balked, suggesting they just discuss whatever it was over the phone, he became insistent."

Jeffrey paused. "In the end," he said at last, "she agreed."

"Mr. Wynn?" The voice belonged to the judge. "I wonder if this would be a good time to excuse the people in the gallery who've asked not to be present when you discuss your overview of the crime."

"Yes, Your Honor. Thank you. I believe it would."

CHAPTER SIXTEEN

Susannah's family knew what the prosecution believed happened to their daughter and grandson, and what the forensic evidence showed. Jeffrey had described it to them privately, in the depth and detail they'd wanted to hear.

He wouldn't be telling the jury anything the family didn't know.

They simply didn't want to hear it again.

Jeffrey had reassured them about their decision to leave the courtroom. It wasn't a betrayal of Susannah. It was what she would've wanted them to do.

His smile, when his eyes met Dorothy's as she stood, gently reaffirmed that what they were doing was right.

Only when they'd left the courtroom, and were probably nearing the bank of elevators at the end of the hall, did he address the jury again.

"That Saturday evening, the defendant

and Susannah went by speedboat to the Yarrow Bay Grill. We don't know what was said during their short trip across the lake. Once they were inside the restaurant, the events of the evening are well documented. And, because of increased media attention in the weeks since the defendant had gotten the network job, his public engagement made the evening news — with photographs like this."

It was a perfect engagement photo. The couple, seated at their roses-and-candlelight table, smiling.

"They look happy, don't they?" Jeffrey asked. "That's certainly the impression most of the witnesses took away. Some will tell you that Susannah seemed uncomfortable in the beginning. But she relaxed. The defendant said unheard things to her that apparently startled her at first, and eventually made her smile. He'd planned to pop the question — have the cake pop it for him — at the end of the meal. But in a voice that was easily overheard, he told the maître d' he couldn't wait. Sparkling cider appeared first. No alcohol, the defendant announced, for the pregnant mom. Or, he added, for the father who was driving the speedboat.

"When the cake arrived, the defendant got

down on one knee. The defense will probably show you a number of photographs of this scene. The maître d' wasn't the only one in the restaurant with a camera. The cake did the asking. But the defendant also had a request. 'Please don't break my heart,' he said, 'in front of all these people.'

"She didn't."

Jeffrey gestured to the photograph. "The defense wants you to believe in this photograph. They want you to find it impossible to reconcile with what happens a few hours later. The state wants you to believe in this photograph, too. Not the invisible promises of happily ever after, but what's visible here. What's real. This photograph marks the beginning of the trail of evidence Susannah left for you. Had she known how important your view of her neck and shoulders would be, she might have worn a revealing blouse."

Jeffrey stopped. Abruptly.

"No," he said, "I'm wrong. Had Susannah Nichols known what the defendant had in store for her, she'd gladly have spent the rest of her life in hiding to save her baby boy."

Jeffrey stopped again as emotion threatened. Glenn and Dorothy Nichols weren't alone in having difficulty with this part of his opening statement. He'd known it would be tough — and that he must keep the emotion he felt out of his voice.

This was Susannah's story. Intrusion of any emotion other than what she must have experienced as she fought for her life — her baby's life — diminished, not enhanced, its power.

"You'll see this photograph again later, and in close-up. But this is good enough to show you what's not there. There are no bruises on her collarbone. Or on her neck. *No bruises.* The blouse Susannah chose to wear on the evening of her murder allows you to know that critical truth.

"You'll see her bruises, later, in the photographs I've told you I won't be showing you today — but which, when I do, I'll ask you to examine closely, and unflinchingly. For Susannah."

Jeffrey clicked the remote, and the projector shut down.

The slide show was over.

"You'll hear two very different versions of what happened that night. In some cases, there's a middle ground between the defense's take on events, and what the prosecution believes occurred. That's not the situation here. We believe the murder of Susannah and Matthew Nichols was a carefully planned cold-blooded killing. Premeditated, ladies and gentlemen, and — almost — perfectly executed."

Jeffrey looked at the jury and saw what he had hoped to see. They were with him, listening to every word. What followed would be a little complicated. The two versions of what happened that night. Their expressions told him he'd have their full attention throughout the intricate journey.

"The defense maintains her death was accidental. At about 1:00 a.m., they'll tell you, Susannah left the bed where she and the defendant had been sleeping, and where he was still asleep. She went outside to make a cell phone call to someone with whom she wanted to share the happy news. No calls were made. But, at about 1:00 a.m., the phone's power was turned on.

"There's a cleat on the dock, to which the speedboat was tied. While scanning the directory perhaps, she tripped on the cleat. She fell forward, the defense will say, dropping her cell phone onto the dock and striking her head on the boat. She lost consciousness, slipped into the water and drowned."

Jeffrey paused. Unnecessarily. The jurors' faces assured him they were with him — and were eager to hear more.

"The defense will show you the defendant's videotaped interview with the police conducted four hours after Susannah's body was recovered. We'll show it to you, too. According to the interview, the defendant awakened alone at dawn. He wasn't immediately concerned. Susannah's clothes were where she'd left them, and the door was ajar. Susannah had worn one of his football jerseys to bed. Despite her pregnancy, it was loose on her, big on her. She'd have felt comfortable wearing it outside. That's where she'd be, he decides. Watching the sunrise.

"But he can't find her. When he spots her cell phone on the dock, he looks toward the water — and sees blood on the speedboat. He calls her. Shouts her name. Early-morning kayakers hear him. His neighbors do, too. By the time they reach him, he's in the water. The police are called. Maritime rescue is called. At eight-fifty-three, divers find Susannah underneath the houseboat.

"A tragic accident, the defense will tell you."

Jeffrey signaled the end of the first version, the false version, with a casual gesture toward the defense table. His gaze didn't follow his gesture and, although a few jurors did look at the defendant, they quickly returned to Jeffrey. They wanted to hear the second version of events . . . the one, Jeffrey had told them, he believed the evidence would prove to be true.

"Here's what the state says on Susannah's behalf. Her killer learned well from the mistakes of others who chose murder as a means of escaping the responsibilities of fatherhood. There'd be no far-fetched alibis from him. No secret girlfriends. No ridiculous suggestions that a murderous stranger — much less a van full of strangers — happened by.

"This killer, this defendant, placed himself squarely at the scene of the crime. In his own home. He was there, he claimed, asleep when the tragedy occurred. It was a clever plan, and a methodical one. And, as I've said, it was almost perfectly executed. If not for Susannah, he might have gotten away with it."

Jeffrey paused before repeating, "If not for Susannah."

He paused a second time, then began again. "Here's what the state believes the evidence will prove. We know that Susannah and the defendant went to bed. They didn't make love. We know that, too. The defendant says, on the videotape, that they held each other, talked, fell asleep. Maybe that's true.

"At about 1:00 a.m., the defendant convinced her to go outside with him. It wouldn't have taken much persuasion. It was warm. And, on the moonless night Susannah died, the sky was filled with shooting stars, the meteor showers we see in Seattle every August. He led her toward the speedboat, stopping when he reached the spot he'd selected near the cleat. He moved behind her, touching her, getting her to relax, to feel safe.

"Then he shoved her toward the boat. And made the critical mistake. The blow needed to render her unconscious. She would've drowned without a struggle. Our crime scene investigators would have been troubled that such a powerful blow could have resulted from tripping over a cleat. Force would've been used, they'd have told us. Someone pushed her from behind. In an attempt to convince the prosecutor's office to move forward with the case, they would've generated the same diagrams that you'll see. The diagrams are important and, we believe, irrefutable. Had Susannah fallen instead of being shoved, her head would've struck the hull significantly closer to the dock, and there wouldn't have been nearly as much blood.

"We wouldn't have needed convincing about the truth of the crime. But we have a responsibility to the taxpayers to prosecute cases in which the verdict we're seeking is a reasonable outcome of the trial. I honestly don't know if we'd be here if Susannah had drowned without a fight. If, without her fighting, we would've had sufficient proof.

"I can tell you," he continued, "we'd have *wanted* to be here. What I can't tell you is why the defendant failed to inflict the degree of head trauma he'd planned. A last-second shred of conscience? That's possible, I suppose. A simple miscalculation is more likely. The defendant may have overestimated how powerful he was.

"Susannah entered the water stunned but conscious. He dove in after her. The struggle was fierce. Susannah fought hard. She couldn't win. But she could leave evidence that would identify her killer.

"I have no idea how the defense plans to explain the bruises she sustained when the defendant pushed her down — and held her down. Hands made the bruises. Large hands. The defendant's hands.

"Maybe the defense won't deny who made the bruises, only *how* they were made. With affection, they'll try to tell you. Not with violence. But you'll see for yourself the violence in her bruises. And forensic specialists will show you why these are perimortem bruises, made *while* Susannah was dying, not bruises made in bed a few hours before."

For the first time during his opening statement, Jeffrey directed his comments not to the jury, but to the man who'd killed. His comments, and his gaze. "The defendant, Kevin Beale, murdered Susannah Nichols. And, in murdering Susannah, he murdered Matthew, too. That's what the state believes. And what the evidence will show. We're not required to show motive. There's a reason for this. Some killers simply kill. For others, the reasons are so impossible to fathom, a jury might reject them as viable motives and set the killers free."

Kevin Beale wasn't going to meet his gaze. Under instruction, perhaps, from Marteen. That was all right. The remainder of his remarks were to the jury. Had Kevin Beale dared to lock eyes with him, Jeffrey would have been loath to turn away.

"We have motive here," he said to the jury. "Unfathomable in my view and, I would imagine, in yours. How could any man murder his unborn child? But some men, some sociopaths, do. And those men blame their victims. It's the woman's fault for getting pregnant — even though she didn't get there alone. And the baby's fault, too, for being conceived. The killer's burdened with a responsibility he doesn't want. To him, this egocentric man without a conscience, there's only one way to get rid of the obstacles that have placed themselves — again, *their* fault — between him and his freedom. He has to kill them. That's what they deserve. This defendant, the man on trial for the murders of a vibrant young woman and her innocent unborn son, summarized his predicament for you. What *choice* did he have? That's how he put it."

As Jeffrey looked at the men and women who would decide Kevin Beale's fate, he felt a surge of the emotion he'd so resolutely kept in check.

"You'll have a choice, too, at the end of this trial. I'm asking you now, just as I'll ask you in closing, to make that choice based on the truth of what you'll hear."

CHAPTER SEVENTEEN

Tuesday, April 12
Noon
Baby girl, baby girl!

You're our healthy daughter. You know this. You've known it all along. That's why you've been smiling.

Now we know it, too. You should see your dad, how relieved he is, how worried he was, how much worry he was hiding from me.

But he's floating now. Just like you — and me. Floating and daring to dream.

Kathleen gave us a snapshot from your ultrasound. I scanned it into the computer, did a little framing and trimming, then printed a wallet-sized photo, so you can be with him all the time.

He needs your optimism. The trial's in its third week, and the media's being soooo critical of what he's presented so far. They loved his opening statement, and even though he's doing exactly what he promised, revealing the story as it unfolded, they're getting impatient.

They want the Perry Mason moment (which, in the real world, doesn't exist). Your dad's doing what he must. Slowly, surely, *brilliantly* putting the necessary testimony into the record.

And you're helping him. I can see it — you — in his tired eyes, even on TV. A deep, steady glow. It's there, you're there, always. No matter how intently he's concentrating on what Marteen is doing to a prosecution witness on cross-exam. (I'm amending that to *trying to do.* Your dad has prepared his witnesses well. Even the restless pundits admit the defense has been thwarted in its attempts to impeach their testimony.)

The glow of you never dims. But sometimes it brightens. You sneak into his consciousness when he needs the conscious memory most.

It happened this morning, and I could read his thought. *She's a girl. Our baby's a girl.*

I told you it didn't matter. And it didn't. Doesn't. We want *you.*

But I feel even closer to you now, and I would've thought it wasn't possible to feel any closer.

Do I have advice to give you? Mother to daughter?

Undoubtedly I do.

You'll make your own path, of course. But I hope you'll let your mom make a suggestion or two along the way.

At the moment, sweet girl, you're a captive audience, held securely — and I hope gently — by me.

So, what shall I tell you here and now?

Nothing, it seems. I'm unaccountably stalled. Writer's block. Or mother's block, confronted as I am with the profound responsibility of imparting sage advice.

Or maybe it's the memory of giving unwanted advice — to Meg.

I know what Meg would say about advice. If you can't be a role model, be a cautionary tale. She says it laughingly, but I wonder . . .

We've been seeing each other, and/or talking to each other, *every* day. About you, of course. And the trial. We watch it in our respective homes and, when Marteen does something particularly slimy, we both reach for the phone.

"I hate him!" she said yesterday. "Can't Judge Owens just say enough is enough, the sociopath is clearly guilty, I'm issuing a verdict from the bench? Oh, and just on general principles, while I'm at it, I'm throwing in a few life sentences for Marteen." Then she sighed loudly. "I know Jeffrey wants a fair verdict. He's such a law-and-order purist. But I'll take

188

a conviction any way we can get it."

Meg believes your dad *will* get the conviction. And, unlike the media, she's not restless. She finds the testimony interesting, and important. She listens to every word . . . and, as we agreed, she lets your dad know how the witnesses — and attorneys — are coming across. She insists her objectivity is intact. She says your dad really is a gentleman — which, of course, he is — and Marteen is, well, *not.*

My sister was going to be a surrogate "incubator" for me.

She's become a surrogate juror for your dad. Her insight is invaluable, he says. He's tried saying it to her. She doesn't like to hear it. Because of that uneasiness with compliments she's always had.

I'm worried that it's more than uneasiness. That she feels undeserving, somehow. Unworthy of being praised.

Just like I'm worried that, laughingly though she says it, she truly views herself as a cautionary tale.

A conversation we had on Saturday makes me wonder all the more.

We were shopping for maternity clothes. (Having Meg along means I now have some very fashionable ones.) I was talking about you, happy chatter, when I noticed the sweetest expression on her face.

"What, Meg?" I asked.

"Do you hear the way your voice changes whenever you talk about the baby?"

"It does?" I replied.

"Oh, yes," she told me. "It changes when you talk about Jeffrey, too. Not every time. Not when it's a discussion, for example, of his battles with Marteen. But anytime the topic is the least bit personal."

"When I'm talking about him and the baby, I suppose."

"Yes, but you've always had your Jeffrey voice — your in-love-with-Jeffrey voice. And now you have your in-love-with-the-baby voice. They're a little different, but variations on a theme."

The in-love theme, baby girl. I'm in love with you both.

"Don't you hear it?" Meg wondered.

"No. Well, I guess I've never listened. I feel it, though. Everything changes. Brightens. I find myself wishing everyone in the world could be as happy as Jeffrey and me. . . . I'd settle for *you* being as happy, Meg."

She laughed. "I'd settle for being even a fraction as happy." Her smile went away. "I'm working on it, Caroline."

"What does that mean?"

"I'm thinking a lot about who I am and why I

do what I do — and, most of all, how I can fix it."

"Fix what?" I remember saying. "Meg, there's nothing wrong with you!"

"We *both* know that's not true."

I was stunned by the certainty of her words. *So* stunned that instead of asking what she meant, I just said, "I don't know it."

"Yes," Meg insisted, "you do. You, of all people . . . Anyway, I'm working on it."

"Can I help?"

"Maybe, when the time comes, when I have something coherent to say."

"I'm here," I said.

I hope she knows that. I hope, when my sister needs reminding how remarkable she is, she'll come to me. She's such a free spirit, creative and bold, living an imaginative life of her own design.

Your mom, by contrast, is pure paint-by-number.

I'm so lucky your dad wandered onto my canvas. Your dad, and you, and at last I'm sensing a bit of mom-baby wisdom to bestow.

Be kind, my darling, to all living things. This is totally unnecessary advice, isn't it? I know you will be. I also know you'll shower special kindness on those less fortunate than you.

You'll have the world's best role model — your dad — as far as kindness is concerned.

A second bit of advice is coming to me now, and it's as superfluous as the first. It is, after all, what you do.

Smile.

There's science that reinforces the beneficial effects of smiling, both for the smiler and the one who's smiled upon. The smiler's mood lifts, and she looks and feels younger, and those touched by her sunshine feel happier, too.

So there you are, baby girl. My totally unnecessary advice to you. You already smile, and you will be kind.

And that, in the advice department, is it. Do you know what an "advice to my daughter" essay would've looked like six months ago? Pages and pages, volumes and volumes, draft upon draft.

But with you inside me, the complicated becomes simple, and the cluttered becomes clear.

You. My *three*-month-old. You're opening and closing your tiny fists these days, and your little baby mouth.

You're fully formed now. The *you* you'll be. In miniature — but *you.*

All we have to do, from here on, is let you grow.

No problem. Grow you will!

I've thought a lot about what's happened

inside me these past three months, the universe of cells following the complex blueprint created by the union of your dad's DNA and mine.

Any comparison to a manmade creation is preposterous. Presumptuous. There is no comparison.

But architect that I am, I can't help noting the differences.

Your cells went to work immediately. No goofing off.

And no oversight was required. Each cell knew its job, and did it.

There weren't any of the on-site squabbles builders and architects know all too well. Electricians grumbling that the paint's still wet. Carpenters traipsing across not-quite-set tile.

And there weren't roofers wishing they were plumbers, either.

Each cell accepted its destiny, and went about its task. *Joyfully.*

I get to be a toe! A fingernail! An eyelash! A nose!

Miracle isn't word enough to describe a process that creates a baby girl nestled beneath her mother's heart.

No word is.

CHAPTER EIGHTEEN

Thursday, May 12
8:30 a.m.
Dear love,

You have a name! That doesn't sound like news, does it? You already have many names — terms of endearment — and that's before we've even met you.

There'll be many more endearments for you. And I believe I can safely bet that some will persist longer than you might choose — like forever.

Are you making a face at the prospect of your mom and dad calling you "baby girl" on prom night? You're of an age — four months! — to make such faces.

You yawn, too, and stretch your six-inch four-ounce body, and you suck your thumb.

The name that's news is your birth-certificate name. We've also come up with a nickname.

Don't peek. I want you to know the reason

for your name before learning what it is.

I'd planned on the methodical approach. I'd buy every baby-name book ever written, generate a "possibilities" list, and every night, after we'd recapped the day's trial events, I'd say a name to your dad, and he'd say it back to me, and back and forth we'd go, testing it, and talking about how it would feel for you.

We did do that for a while. It was nice. Talking about you is always nice.

When your name came to me, I was nowhere near a baby-name book. I knew it was *your* name. And when I said it to your dad last night, he knew it, too.

We're naming you for your great-grandmother. She's the reason we met, and, from the start, she's believed in our love.

Her name — and your first name — is Roberta. Isn't that beautiful? We think so, and hope you do, too.

Your middle name is Margaret. Aunt Meg's given name.

Your namesakes are thrilled. We called them both, bright and early this morning. They're also delighted by all the nickname options Roberta Margaret has to offer you — and those who love you.

We've already given you a nickname. Like the name itself, when it came to us, it felt preordained.

So, are you ready?

Drum roll, please.

Introducing Miss Roberta Margaret Wynn — otherwise known as Bobbi.

CHAPTER NINETEEN

Monday, May 16
9:30 a.m.
Bobbi love,

I'm feeling a bit blah today. Are you?

Your smile's there. But a little subdued, I think — happy though both of us are that the trial's finally going so well. Maybe we're simply smiled out.

Oh, Bobbi, how the thought of your smile being even slightly subdued makes me ache.

I don't want you to be sad. Ever.

I've decided we'll spend the morning in bed. How decadent is that? But we deserve it. I've made such progress on my work projects I'll have completed everything within a matter of weeks.

You're responsible for the progress. You've helped me make my clients so happy with the coziness of their prospective new homes there's minimal blueprint revising to do. And on top of assisting me with my work, you've attended to your own building project, becoming bigger, stronger, every day.

Having made such excellent progress, we're entitled to luxuriate beneath the covers if we like.

We'll rest, and write in our journal, and listen to the birds. And, if the spirit moves us, we may even do a little shopping from the comfort of our pillows.

This spring, as I do every spring, I spent quite a bit of time admiring the tulips, daffodils, hyacinths in our across-the-street neighbor's garden.

We'll never have Betsy's garden. But I think it's time for a flower garden of our own.

The bulb companies are making it easy. I have stacks of catalogs. The bulbs will arrive for fall planting, and will bloom next spring.

Seattle can be warm in autumn, warm by Seattle standards, anyway. You may be able to enjoy a little autumn sunshine while you and your dad watch me dig.

Of course, he'll offer to do the digging. And planting. I don't believe I'll let him. Exercise will be good for me around about then, and he'll want to hold you whenever he can.

I'll want that for him.

I already do.

I have these blissful months of holding you

around the clock. I wish I could give him even a second of this time. He'd know, in a second, how extraordinary it is.

I tell him what it feels like, but how can one describe the indescribable?

There are symptoms, which *could* be described. And which, in other contexts, might well be viewed as less than desirable. But every symptom, from the whirlies to a new-found passion for peanut butter and pickles (together! on bread!), is proof that you're flourishing.

And playing, I think. Having all kinds of fun.

My body's changing visibly — and invisibly — to accommodate you. It's the invisible changes I've been reading about that intrigue me most. (The visible ones are what the exercise of autumn bulb planting will be designed to reverse.)

I'm immunosuppressed. All pregnant women are. The immune suppression isn't as profound, my reading tells me, as what happens in patients with AIDS. It's closer to what transplant recipients undergo. They're given steroids — and other immunosuppressive medications — to prevent rejection of the foreign tissue they've received.

I'm getting steroid therapy, thanks to you. My adrenal glands are producing extra cortisol to prevent my immune system from treating you as foreign.

Astonishing, isn't it? And counterintuitive. We're one, you and I. There isn't a single tiny thing that's foreign about you — emotionally, anyway . . . just as your dad and I are emotionally one.

Half your DNA is his (lucky girl). But as close as he and I are, and as bonded in our love, if my immune system weren't under a cortisol blockade, it would view his DNA as foreign and launch an assault.

I don't feel immunosuppressed, this morning's blahs notwithstanding. I've never felt healthier. But like all pregnant women, I'm at risk for certain infections I'd otherwise handle with ease.

I find that fascinating, not troubling. I'm being careful. The immunosuppression is more testament to the extraordinary intricacies of creating the miracle of you.

I've wandered as usual, surrendered to the flow of my liquid gel pen and meandering thoughts. We could be sipping lemonade and drifting down a lazy river . . . named *denial.* (An old line, but one I've always liked.)

Okay. I admit it. I'm avoiding a particular thought. A worry. At least I was avoiding it until a second ago.

And now? Dealing with it would be an excellent use of this blah morning — especially since Meg is coming over this afternoon.

To talk, she says. It's time.

She sounds so serious, and so worried.

In the months before I became pregnant with you, on nights when I was feeling especially tired and discouraged, I'd let myself imagine upsetting conversations Meg and I might have — conversations in which I'd learn that she felt as negatively toward me now as she did when we were teens.

I don't believe that anymore. But my emotions haven't caught up to what I know is true. Pavlovian conditioning, I suppose. (You'll know about Pavlov someday. You'll think it's funny when someone asks, "Does the name Pavlov ring a bell?")

My wariness hasn't gone away. It won't, on its own, and it needs to — ideally before Meg and I talk this afternoon.

My mission, therefore, is to make it go away . . . by putting what Meg said to me on that long-ago April afternoon in its proper perspective.

The memory has gotten huge over the years. Monstrous. I need to whittle it down to size and see it for what it was: an emotional exchange between teenage sisters a lifetime ago.

See it.

Relive it.

Repackage it.

In short, follow the advice any problem-solving expert would give. Sounds reasonable, doesn't it?

Here goes. . . .

It was April sixteenth. My college acceptances had arrived the day before. I'd applied to two schools, the University of Washington, where I planned to go, and Massachusetts Institute of Technology, where I'd applied as a favor to the career counselor at school.

No one else from my high school was applying to MIT. I wouldn't be competing against a classmate for a slot. I had a good chance of getting in, the counselor said. It would be a plus for our school, even if I declined to go.

I knew I'd decline. It was more important than ever to remain close to Meg.

Our mother had emerged from her postdivorce funk with a vengeance. She'd slimmed down, invested in tucks and enhancements, and after a single-minded prowl for a wealthy man to marry, she'd snagged herself one of the city's richest.

They were getting married that June, and would live in his lakefront mansion until Meg graduated from high school. They'd move to California after that. Meg wouldn't go with them. She wouldn't leave Seattle, she said.

I knew our mother and her new husband

would travel while Meg was in high school and, even when they were in town, our mother would be paying less attention to Meg than ever, at a time — boys, cars, alcohol — when Meg needed a mother most.

I *wanted* to remain close to Meg. Yes, it was a struggle of wills, and there was the perpetual worry that something terrible might happen to her. Terrible — but foreseeable, if only I was as vigilant as I should be.

Meg was my sister, and I loved her.

Meg learned about my acceptance at MIT. It was big news at school. She also learned I was planning to decline. It was easy for her to figure out why.

Needless to say, she didn't view my decision as a loving one. According to her, it proved how mean I really was, how hell-bent on ruining her life.

Hadn't I harangued her long enough? Did I have any idea how much she hated me? How she'd been praying I'd be accepted at MIT and leave her alone?

How weird was I, anyway, to derive so much pleasure from tormenting her? I wasn't her mother and had no right to pretend I was. She felt sorry for any children I might have.

Especially a daughter. (Yes, Bobbi, she said that.)

On second thought, she added, she needn't

worry about babies. No man would ever want a woman as rigid as me.

It was a short outburst, like automatic gunfire, brief but devastating. I'm pretty sure I whispered, "I'm sorry."

I don't think I told her I loved her. It would've fallen on deaf ears even if I'd shouted it.

And that was that.

And there it is. A decades-old outburst I *do not* believe is lurking beneath the surface, waiting to recur.

Don't believe . . . but fear. *Still.*

Okay. I know it for what it was. And I've relived it.

At this point, I should be ready for the repackaging — the *shrink*-wrapping, to something small, inconsequential, easily tossed away.

But that's assuming that in reliving it, I've reduced it from larger-than-life to life-sized.

I haven't.

Fine. I'll give it another whirl, accompanied by slow deep breaths and the songs of happy birds outside the window. . . .

. . . No luck. There's another approach. It doesn't feel terribly promising. But it's what we're left with.

The idea is to find a positive consequence of the negative event — a silver lining, in other words, to the dark cloud.

I'm a Virgo. This isn't our forte. On the contrary, Virgos are quite capable of shrouding silver clouds in black.

Determination's also a Virgo trait.

And I'm determined to conquer this.

So. As a result of what Meg said, I didn't give the valedictory address at graduation. From a positive-consequence standpoint, that meant I didn't have to spend the next six weeks worrying about it. I told my teachers I'd changed my mind, without explaining why. How could I give an inspirational address to my classmates when I'd failed so miserably with Meg?

I left Seattle, as Meg wanted me to, and attended MIT. I was unhappy there — because of Meg — for quite a while.

Unhappy, Caroline thought. And self-punishing.

And trying to prove Meg wrong about the rigid girl Meg had said she was and would always be. She could have fun, *be* fun, couldn't she?

In the fall of her freshman year, Caroline followed a stream of other co-eds from her dormitory to an off-campus party. For the first time in her life, she drank. And, also a first, had sex.

Unprotected sex. With a boy whose last name she never learned, and who probably wasn't a student at MIT. She'd spent the next few months on the lookout for him — so she could turn away before he spotted her — but never saw him again.

She also spent the next few months ignoring an ache in her lower abdomen. Did she know it was a raging infection? One that would burn itself out only after causing such scarring to her Fallopian tubes that, short of major medical advances, she'd be unable to conceive?

Maybe she knew it. Sensed it.

And was punishing herself for having failed so miserably with Meg.

She was unhappy then. And for a very long time.

But not forever. (Maybe we're getting somewhere.)

In my junior year, I signed up for a department of architecture course entitled Introduction to Design Computing. It was the "computing" not the "design" aspect that attracted me. At the time, I was a double major in computer science and math.

I loved design computing. Loved design. And decided to become an architect instead of the computer programmer I thought I'd be.

I worked in Manhattan for a while. Designing ultramodern buildings. Winning a number of awards. That was positive in itself. More importantly, it made me employable elsewhere.

I'd never been to Denver. But I was homesick. Denver wasn't home. But it was closer than I'd been in years, and as close as I dared to be.

Several Denver firms were interested in hiring me. I made my choice because of a specific project one of them was involved in — the design of a new wing for the art museum.

Guess whose grandmother was on the museum's architectural committee?

And guess who she, Roberta, invited to a museum-related party in her home, and *insisted* that her very busy prosecutor-attorney grandson also attend?

She knew, Bobbi, your namesake *knew* that your dad and I were meant to be.

And, Caroline thought, Roberta wanted our love to be.

The rest of Jeffrey's family was more reserved.

Happy marriages abounded in the many branches of the Wynn family's sprawling tree. They acknowledged divorce as an unfortunate — yet sometimes necessary — eventuality. In certain instances, they knew, the dissolution of a marriage was for the best.

To them, the divorce of Caroline's parents was not, in itself, a cause for alarm. The disintegration of her family was.

Jeffrey's parents liked Caroline and wished her well — just not with their son. Jeffrey could have any woman he wanted. Why borrow trouble by getting involved with someone with such an emotionally unstable pedigree?

Because I'm in love with her, Jeffrey replied. She's the only woman I will ever love.

Roberta embraced the marriage. The others accepted it.

Caroline's infertility hadn't helped. Neither did the presumed chlamydial infection that had caused it — and that was without their knowing the sordid details Caroline had revealed to Jeffrey.

Then came Jeffrey's decision to move to Seattle because he knew how important it was for the woman he loved to reunite with the sister from whom she was estranged.

There was no point in sharing her in-laws' uncertainties with Bobbi.

Roberta Margaret Wynn's grandparents

— and great grandmother — would love Bobbi as exuberantly as they'd always loved Jeffrey.

Besides, Caroline realized, it had finally appeared.

The silver lining . . .

We were meant to be, Bobbi. And because of your dad's love, I came to believe that I could be a mom, after all.

And now, precious Bobbi, we have you.

It doesn't get more silvery than that.

If not for Meg, none of it would have happened. *You* wouldn't have happened.

Her insistence that I'd ruined her life ended up saving mine.

And now I'm wondering if there's even more happiness hidden in that unhappy day.

What if Meg said what she did to free me from the responsibility, which perhaps she viewed as a burden, of watching over her?

What if her terrible words came from love, not hate?

That kind of generosity would be *so* Meg, and —

Bobbi? *Bobbi?*

Meg was pacing. And practicing. Saying aloud what she was going to tell Caroline today. The problem was, the words changed with each rehearsal.

Meg's pacing had taken her close to the phone when it rang.

"Meg? Bobbi moved!"

"Oh, Caroline. Tell me."

"I woke up feeling blah and decided to spend a lazy morning in bed. Now I think that she was behind the blahness. She wanted my undivided attention when she made her grand entrance."

"And she had it."

"Oh, yes."

"And it *was* grand?"

"So grand, Meg. And so different from what I expected. I'd been anticipating her moving. I knew it was due to happen any day. I imagined a fluttering, I suppose, and thought it would be so subtle I'd have trouble deciding if it was Bobbi or me."

"But that's not what happened."

"Not even close. There wasn't the slightest ambiguity about it, Meg. It felt like a seismic shift. The jolt that announces the earthquake. It was Bobbi. *Bobbi.* Not me."

"Have you told Jeffrey?"

"I left a voice message. He and the judge and Marteen are in some mysterious emergency meeting. Sheila had no idea what it was about. Maybe Marteen realizes his case is in serious trouble and wants to work out some kind of plea."

"Would Jeffrey do that?"

"I suppose it depends on what it was."

"I'm so glad you called me, Caroline."

"*Of course* I called you."

"Well. Thank —"

"Don't even think about thanking me for anything, Meg Gallagher. Ever!"

"Okay. Maybe I shouldn't come over this afternoon? If you're feeling blah?"

"The blahs are gone, now that Bobbi's made her grand hello. Come over anytime, Meg. Whenever's good for you. Bobbi and I will be right here."

CHAPTER TWENTY

"Come in!" Caroline said when Meg arrived a half hour later.

"Any more action from Bobbi?"

"Not a single aftershock. She's resting, I think. But," Caroline said softly, "I'm sensing her presence in a way I haven't before. Bobbi as Bobbi, distinct from me."

"A woman in her own right?"

"Absolutely. And a force to be reckoned with."

They chatted about Bobbi, and chatted about Bobbi, until — with an expectant glance from Caroline, answered with a nervous shrug from Meg — both acknowledged they'd put off Meg's reason for today's visit long enough.

Caroline sat while she listened.

Meg paced while she talked. "I told you I was trying to figure out why I am who I am, and why I do what I do. Well, I have. I guess I should explain what I'm referring to . . .

even though you already know."

"I *do* know. You're kind, loving —"

"No, Caroline. I need to tell you. Here's who I am: someone who runs away from emotion. And here's what I do: hurt the people I love. Drive them away."

"Are you talking about Mark?"

Caroline's question halted Meg's pacing midstride. "Mark?"

"Remember when you told me about my in-love-with-Jeffrey voice? You had a different voice, an in-love voice, too, when you talked about Mark. You still have that voice. I heard it just now. I also know how happy you were with him. That happiness went away after you broke up. You never gave much of a reason for what happened, and I never really pushed. I didn't feel comfortable cross-examining you . . . then."

"But now you do?"

Meg's question brimmed with hope, as if, in her definition of loving sisters, cross-examining one another was expected, welcomed, without fear.

"Now," Caroline replied, "I do. I need to tell you, first, about Mark. He had an in-love voice, too, for you. And the way he looked at you . . . I saw him, Meg. The night I miscarried. I was so out of it, I didn't acknowledge him. But he was there, helping me, saying reassuring things. He would've been just as gentle, as reassuring, no matter who I was. But *because* of who I was, whose sister I was, hints of his voice for you, and his look for you, trickled in. I saw his love, Meg, and how sad he is without you. So, when you're talking about running away from emotion, and hurting someone you love, you're talking about Mark, aren't you?"

"About Mark," Meg said. Hesitated. Breathed. "And about you."

"I'm right here, Meg. Mark would be, too. If you wanted him to be."

"I do . . . and I don't. Because of who I am . . ."

"You're a kind, loving — okay!" Caroline smiled. "We'll get to that later. You said you've figured out why you're the way you *think* you are."

"I have. It's actually pretty simple. And pretty pathetic. It's also something you'd suppose I'd have gotten over years, *decades,* ago." Meg looked from her sister's reassuring face to the carpeted living-room floor. "It happened, after all, when I was six."

"When you were six? Oh, Meg, did someone . . . were you sexually —"

"*No,* Caroline." It was Meg's turn to do the reassuring. "Nothing horrific like that. That's probably why I've always assumed there had to be something *more.*"

"So you've known about whatever it is?"

"All this time? Yes. No repressed memories for me. No ominous gaps in the story of my life. The memory's always been vivid. I've just refused to admit it could've had such a lasting effect. I mean, you overhear your parents saying hurtful things about you. So what? You get over it. Sticks and stones — et cetera."

"You overheard our parents saying hurtful things about *you?* But —" Caroline's voice held not a trace of envy "— you were their golden girl."

"Their tarnished girl, actually. I polished up nicely for their friends. A crowd-pleaser every time."

"I thought you enjoyed performing."

"I did," Meg said. "I loved pleasing the parents I loved, and who I believed loved me."

"They did love you, Meg, to the extent they were capable of loving anyone but themselves. Not that that's a ringing endorsement of them. They were selfish. Self-absorbed. What did you hear them say?"

"They were angry, arguing. He was telling her he'd had enough, wanted out of the marriage, *was* getting out of it. He only wished he'd left when he wanted to, before

I was born. She'd apparently convinced him to stay by acknowledging the problems they'd had — and promising a solution. Me. What better way to rediscover their love than with a new baby? The trouble was, I wasn't the baby she'd promised him . . . the perfect baby *you'd* been. I was difficult from the moment they brought me home. I cried, screamed, throughout the night."

"I don't remember that, Meg."

"You were only four when I was born."

"I don't remember ever seeing you cry."

"I pretty much gave up crying after overhearing them that day."

"I *hate* them." Caroline's words were uncomplicated, her emotions pure and true.

"And they hated me. I was an imperfect baby who got worse with age. I was a 'terror' to quote Dad, and 'unlovable' according to Mom. I was supposed to save their marriage. Instead I became its final straw."

"A baby shouldn't be born with a job," Caroline said, recalling one of several framed quotations on the Reproductive Medicine Clinic's waiting room wall. That particular quote was attributed to Dr. Phil McGraw. "But that *is* what our defective parents did to you. It was your job to fix a marriage that was hopelessly broken. I can't believe this! How *dare* they blame you? I'm so sorry, Meg. It's no wonder this has stayed with you all these years. You were a little girl. They were your world. You depended on them, loved them, trusted them. And they betrayed you. Did they know you overheard what they were saying?"

"No. I had an upset stomach and decided to skip dance class after school. They weren't putting on a show for me, Caroline, hoping I'd mend my ways. I tried to mend them, though. I had no idea what I was doing wrong, so I did what I could to be different. I thought it was working, that things *were* better. But a few months later Dad moved out, and that was that."

Meg started to speak again. Stopped.

"What, Meg? What were you going to say?"

"Something I'd never even considered telling you."

"Tell me. Please."

"I was desperate to make things right. I thought if the reason for their troubled marriage went away, if *I* went away . . . I remembered hearing Mom talk about drinking herself to death."

"Oh, Meg." Caroline's voice trembled. "*Meg.* You were trying to kill yourself that night?"

"I was trying to go away. I guess that was the beginning of my tendency to run away. Obviously, at six, I had no real concept of death. I was looking for a solution to a dilemma I'd caused." Meg was causing emotion now. Sadness, such sadness, in the sister she loved. "Caroline! It's okay. You *rescued* me."

Caroline shook her head. "Not really. Not from all the terrible things you believed. You do know you had *nothing* to do with their problems?"

"Sure. Rationally. As an adult. But I made the mistake of assuming that knowledge was power. Recognizing that it was their problem, not mine, was supposed to mean there'd be no lasting effect on me. No such luck. As I've been deconstructing who I am, I keep returning to what happened that day."

"I'm not surprised," Caroline murmured. "Not surprised at all."

"Well, I certainly took what they said to heart. So much so that once the divorce was final and all was lost, I became the unlovable terror they'd already said I was. I'd destroyed their marriage, and my next victim was you."

"Me?"

"I made your life hell, Caroline. We both

know it. Mom washed her hands of me. Why not? I'd ruined her marriage. But you hung in, even though I wasn't worth hanging in for —"

"There's nothing wrong with you, Meg! There never has been! You weren't a terror. And you weren't ever unlovable. You simply — but it's not so simple, is it? — had the great misfortune of being born to self-centered pseudoadults whose first daughter was so bland she required little care or attention." Caroline spoke with a bitterness, an anger, she couldn't quite control.

"You're not bland, Caroline."

"I must've been as an infant. Quiet. Passive. Qualities viewed as ideal in a baby only by the type of lazy, inadequate parents we happened to have."

"Alcoholic parents."

"You think so?"

"I'm pretty sure. The functioning kind. They never *appeared* to be intoxicated. But they drank — a lot. Did you really not notice? I assumed that was why you'd stopped drinking years ago."

"No. I just realized that as much I enjoyed the giddiness of a glass of wine, the short-lived euphoria wasn't really worth it. I'd get sleepy, which wasn't so bad, but the following day I'd feel down. What about you, Meg?"

"I've done way too much drinking for all the wrong reasons. None of which includes the fun of getting giddy. Alcohol hasn't made me feel giddy for years."

"You drink to . . . ?"

"Escape's the clichéd answer. The boring truth. Alcohol helped me run away emotionally and forget — not care — for a while. Feeling down the next day was an acceptable side effect."

"You're talking in the past tense."

"My drinking *is* past tense. Thanks to you."

"If you're sober, Meg, it's thanks to you."

"Only for the past month or so. I stopped in January, when I thought I might be carrying . . . Bobbi. She still would've been Bobbi, wouldn't she? The eleventh embryo would've been your Bobbi."

"Our Bobbi," Caroline said. "Our force to be reckoned with. No matter where she spent her first nine months. You stopped drinking when you thought it might be you."

"Yes. And by the time I'd made it through the surrogacy screening process, you were already pregnant. And dizzy. You needed a sober driver for a while. Somewhere along the line, I decided to see if I could just say no, and keep saying no . . . and, most importantly, figure out why I'd always said yes."

"Now you know."

"And now I wonder how different everything might've been if I hadn't come home that day."

"Our parents weren't subtle. Once they'd decided to blame you for their failure, they would've communicated their displeasure."

"And I would've responded accordingly . . . behaved despicably."

"You never behaved despicably."

"Caroline."

"You were a little wild. With good reason."

"There's never a good reason for being cruel."

"You don't have a cruel bone in your body."

"Come on, Caroline."

"You don't!"

"You know I do. You may have forgiven the hateful things I said to you that April, but you haven't forgotten them."

"You're right. But those words have a marvelous new spin. A silver lining — to use another cliché. Wait here. I'll show you."

On her return, Caroline handed her journal to Meg.

"I don't think either of us could read this

out loud. So just start reading here."

Caroline pointed to the morning's entry, beginning *Bobbi love, I'm feeling a bit blah today* — then watched as her sister read her emotional words.

Meg smiled at flower gardens and pickle sandwiches.

And became thoughtful during Caroline's description of nature's temporary immuno-suppression of pregnant mothers.

And so sad as she read about her teenage outburst Caroline nearly grabbed the journal away.

"Caroline," she whispered, "what I said about hoping you'd never have a daughter —"

"Don't worry about that! We need to look at the forest here, Meg. Not the trees. Keep reading. Please."

She did, without even glancing up until she'd read to the end.

"I wish I'd said those things to make it easier for you to go to MIT. I *wish* it'd been generosity, not cruelty, behind my awful words. But it wasn't."

"I'm not so sure," Caroline said. "But, for the sake of argument, we'll take every word at face value. And in that case, it was frustration speaking. Frustration, Meg. Not cruelty. You'll never get me to buy that. You were fourteen, asserting your own identity the way teenage girls do — by being hyper-critical of their mothers. Since I was the only mother in sight, I was the obvious target. I'm counting on you to pick up the pieces of my broken heart fourteen years from now, when my Bobbi says things like that to me."

"She won't."

"The books say she will. Can I count on you, Meg? To pick up the pieces?"

She nodded, but frowned, as if she'd gotten off way too easily, as if Caroline should have raged at her as she'd raged at Caroline.

Caroline knew Meg hadn't gotten off easily. There'd been nothing easy about living with the casual cruelty inflicted by their parents.

"I'm not giving up on the idea that you wanted me to go to MIT for my own sake. I also think it's possible you were afraid I *wanted* to leave, and maybe would leave, so you decided you'd hurt less if you drove me away. No, *decided* is the wrong word. It would've been an instinct for self-preservation learned when you were six."

"I've been wondering that, too."

"Then wonder no more," she said lightly. "It makes perfect sense."

"Caroline? It didn't hurt less. I missed you. Desperately."

"I missed you, too."

Meg, who never cried, swiped at sudden tears.

"Dammit!" It wasn't a ferocious protest. "Your hormones must be contagious."

"Too bad!" Caroline smiled. "I hope getting rid of monstrous memories is just as contagious. Not that I got rid of my memory of *our* conversation that April afternoon. In retrospect, it wasn't so monstrous — and it has that silver lining I'm not about to throw away. But your memory of what you overheard *is* monstrous. We need to whittle it from huge to life-sized to something that can easily be crushed inside a fist. Two fists. We'll throw it away together."

"What if it has a silver lining, too?"

"I'm not sure how we're going to find anything remotely positive, much less happy, about causing an innocent child such anguish. I don't think we have to worry about inadvertently throwing away a silver lining."

Caroline meant it. Believed it.

But, astonishingly, Meg did not.

And, perhaps, neither did Bobbi. What Caroline felt was softer than a jolt. A gentle kicking steady and sure.

Dancing, Caroline thought.

As Meg had once danced . . . and smiled. Meg was smiling now across the room.

"There *was* a silver lining, Caroline. Their hurtful words gave me you as my mother."

CHAPTER TWENTY-ONE

Monday, May 16
2:45 p.m.

"Kathleen wants me to find a pregnancy buddy," Caroline said. "I was thinking you, if you're game."

They'd been walking in Caroline's neighborhood, a stroll with rhododendrons in the foreground and Rainier, in the distance, glistening white above the lake.

They'd been walking, without talking, for a while.

Without needing to talk.

"I'm game," Meg replied. "Are we doing LaMaze?"

Caroline shook her head. "I'll probably have a C-section. Kathleen's concerned about uterine scarring from my previous miscarriages and D&Cs."

"And your bleeding last August."

"That, too."

"So I'd be with you during the C-section if Jeffrey couldn't be?"

"What Kathleen has in mind is more of a postpartum buddy. Someone — in addition to Jeffrey — on the lookout for depression I might develop following Bobbi's birth. There's a DVD she wants the three of us to watch. She gives it to all her patients. She says it's important for the future mom to know about postpartum depression, and even more important for her family to."

"Because?" Meg asked.

"Women with PPD tend to hide their depression. They don't realize what it is, only that the way they're feeling isn't how a new mother should feel. They're not bonding with the baby. It's bewildering to them, and shameful. The buddy has to agree to be extremely pushy about uncovering hidden worries the new mother might have — and even pushier about making sure she gets help. PPD's treatable, Kathleen says. Easily treatable. And curable."

"With the least provocation," Meg promised, "I will physically load you into the car — and tuck Bobbi into her carseat — and drive you straight to QAMC."

"That's what I was hoping you'd say."

Caroline lifted her face to the warm springtime sun. "I feel so good, Meg. So excited about Bobbi, so bonded with her already, I can't imagine any of that going away. But apparently that's what all deliriously happy pregnant women say — and why the depression's so devastating when it hits."

"Forewarned is forearmed."

Caroline smiled. "Kathleen's sentiments exactly," she said as she retrieved her chiming cell phone from her pocket. "It's Jeffrey," she said, glancing at the call display. "Hi . . . Oh. You haven't picked up my message yet. . . . She moved, Jeffrey. Bobbi *moved.*"

Meg walked a short distance away, to give Caroline and Jeffrey a little privacy. Caroline could have enhanced that privacy by turning. She didn't. And, when the conversation shifted from Bobbi to the reason Jeffrey had called, she walked toward the spot where Meg stood.

It was serious, whatever it was. Caroline frowned as she listened. Eventually she spoke.

"Meg's right here. I'll ask her." Caroline met her eyes. She didn't actually ask; she stated what she believed to be fact. "You don't know Kevin Beale."

"No, I don't. I made pillows for the

houseboat. Weeks before he ever saw it. Why?"

"What about Kevin's friends? Or Susannah's?"

"No. *Why?*"

"I'll explain in a minute." Caroline spoke into the phone again. "She says no, Jeffrey. And if I've ever met anyone involved in the case, it was such a casual encounter I don't remember it — and it wouldn't be of any consequence, anyway. This is *nothing* . . . isn't it? Just Marteen trying to delay the inevitable? . . . I hope so, too . . . That's fine. Really . . . Okay. See you then. I love you."

Caroline closed her cell phone, frowning again. "Turns out Marteen wasn't going for a plea agreement," she told Meg. "He's got a better idea. A mistrial."

"That's not going to happen."

"Marteen thinks it is."

"On what grounds?"

"Prosecutorial misconduct."

"What?"

"He's saying Jeffrey should have recused himself months ago, that he's too personally involved."

"Oh, Caroline. Your miscarriages?"

"No. Not my miscarriages, and not the pillows you made for the houseboat. It's something new. Something that's supposedly come to light since the trial began."

"What?"

"Marteen won't say, and he doesn't have to in advance of tomorrow's hearing. That's what's been scheduled, a hearing before the judge. The jury won't be there, but the television cameras will."

"Judge Owens *must* know this is an act of desperation. The defense got hammered last week. The guilty verdict is practically guaranteed before Marteen even calls his first witness. Marteen knows his only hope is to prevent the jury from hearing what Jeffrey's going to present this week. This is so transparent. And so bogus. I can't believe Judge Owens is going along with it."

"Jeffrey says she's not happy about it. But that she also has no choice. The defense says it has critical information. The judge is obliged to hear it."

"This is going to backfire, Caroline. Marteen will present some ridiculous argument and everyone will see it for the ploy it is. What a waste of time!" She paused. "Jeffrey's not really worried, is he?"

"He is worried, Meg. Courtroom antics are one thing. Insisting on a judicial hearing in the middle of a trial is another. Marteen has a reputation to protect. He's not going to throw it away on frivolous allegations. He has something — or believes he does."

"And he's planning an ambush on live TV."

Caroline nodded. "Jeffrey has between now and nine o'clock tomorrow morning to try to figure out what Marteen has, and prepare for it."

"Prosecutorial misconduct doesn't necessarily mean Jeffrey. It could be anyone in the office who's working on the case."

"That's right. But Marteen's wording to the judge, that Jeffrey should have recused himself because he's too personally involved, sounded pretty specific."

"An excellent way to trick Jeffrey into focusing on himself instead of finding whoever's actually got the conflict," Meg said indignantly. "He's not falling for it, is he?"

"No. Anyone and everyone involved in the case will be at our place at six to spend the evening discussing this."

"So we'd better get hopping," Meg said. "We have pizza to order and coffee to make. I can go out for ice cream, too. Unless you and Bobbi already have enough in your freezer."

Caroline smiled. "We have quite a bit."

Then she sighed.

"I'll help you get everything ready," Meg said. "Then I'll leave. I know I'm an outsider."

"Meg," Caroline said, "you're not an outsider. You're our family." She shook away her look of worry and smiled again. "You're also Jeffrey's secret weapon. He's valued your thoughts and insights on the case. He'll want you there tonight — and tomorrow in court."

CHAPTER
TWENTY-TWO

King County Courthouse
Tuesday, May 17
9:00 a.m.

The courtroom was packed, with overflow in adjacent areas, and the excitement was almost palpable.

A few facts were known. The jury had been excused for the day. The notification had been made the previous afternoon in a conference call from the judge.

A transcript of Judge Owens's admonitions to her jurors had been released to the press. They were to take great care to avoid televison, radio, newspapers, as well casual comments that might be overheard in grocery stores and gyms. Ideally, they should find a good book to read — or, if they preferred, enjoy a marathon of their favorite DVDs.

Today's hearing, the judge had told them,

might or might not be relevant to the trial. If it was relevant, she promised, they'd hear about it from her. Otherwise, they were to regard it as procedural issue with no bearing on the matter before them.

By early evening, and prime-time TV, the barrage of rumors had coalesced into exactly what the defense, who'd leaked them, wanted.

The revelations would be explosive. A mistrial inevitable. Jeffrey Wynn could face disbarment and charges could be filed. Contempt of court. Obstruction of justice. And, if what the legal pundits were hearing was true, even conspiracy to murder after the fact.

Yes, *murder.* According to sources "close to" the defense, Marteen was rethinking his theory of the case.

Maybe the prosecution was right.

Maybe Susannah and Matthew Nichols *had* fallen victim to murder, not accidental drowning, while Marteen's innocent client slept.

It was even possible, those sources confided, that in the course of the hearing, the real killer might be revealed . . . and there'd be a Perry Mason moment, after all.

Because of viewer interest in the hearing, televised coverage commenced thirty minutes before the judge was scheduled to gavel her court to order. Legal commentators were unanimous in describing what they saw during those thirty minutes.

The entire prosecution looked haggard. Including, observers noted, the lead prosecutor's wife and sister-in-law. Haggard. *Exhausted.* But defiant, everyone agreed.

Susannah's family had intended to spend this week in seclusion at the undisclosed location where they'd been staying throughout the trial. They'd known what Jeffrey would be saying — and showing — in the final weeks of the prosecution's case-in-chief. They'd also known what every objective court-watcher had come to believe. The forensic evidence would be the grim icing on the prosecution's cake.

Susannah's family wasn't in seclusion. They were in the front row, next to Caroline and Meg, trying to manage the same stolid expression the prosecution team wore — but unable to pull it off. They were worried and fearful.

By contrast, everyone on the defense side of the aisle looked confident and rested. And so eager to get the proceedings underway they fairly leapt to their feet when the door to the judge's chambers opened and Her Honor appeared.

In the scant seconds it took for Judge Owens to stride briskly to the bench, analysts offered speculation about her state of mind. She had to be unhappy, they said. Until now, the trial had been so clean, so "uncircuslike." In fact, one telecaster wondered, wasn't he seeing her displeasure? Even a world-class poker player, he quipped, registered annoyance when she'd gone all-in with pocket kings, and an ace-on-the-river stole her money away.

The quip had clearly been preplanned. No displeasure could be seen.

That wasn't true of what could be detected in the judge's voice.

"If you've been watching the news," she began, "you probably think you have a clear understanding of why we're here today. If it's the same news I've been watching, you don't. Today's proceeding is a hearing. *Not* a trial. Its purpose is to provide me with information the defense believes I need. Under normal circumstances, I'd hear this information in chambers. But because of the interest in this case, and my certainty that a secret hearing would add fuel to the rumors already raging out of control, I've decided to make today's hearing public."

Judge Owens cleared her throat. The annoyance didn't entirely go away. "As I've stated, this *isn't* a trial. It's a data-gathering process for the limited purpose of determining whether the trial you've all been watching may continue. The hearing won't end with charges being filed. In the event that proves to be necessary, it would fall to another court at another time. I'll be making one decision, and one decision only. And, because it's my decision to make, I'm going to feel free to ask the witnesses any questions I might have. Mr. Wynn and Mr. Marteen are aware of this. I've also asked them to withhold their objections." She looked sternly from one to the other. "If I find a line of questioning to be peripheral, I'll put an end to it myself. Today's witnesses will, of course, be under oath. I don't know who these witnesses will be, or what they'll say. That's what we're going to find out. I do know that, regardless of what I decide to do with the testimony, I'm going to prohibit today's witnesses from speaking to the press until the trial is over. Let me make myself clear. I'm talking about the trial, *Washington v. Kevin Beale,* not this hearing. To make it easy for the witnesses to comply with my order, I'm enjoining the media from any and all contact with them. All right. Mr. Marteen. Please proceed."

The defense counsel appeared delighted

to. "Thank you, Your Honor. It has come to our attention that a substantial conflict of interest exists for Mr. Wynn — one he should have disclosed. So significant is the conflict that it's the position of the defense that he should have recused himself from any involvement in the case within days, if not hours, of Susannah Nichols's death. There's even the possibility that what Mr. Wynn did — and didn't do — goes beyond an undisclosed conflict."

"Mr. Marteen."

"Yes, Your Honor."

"I don't need an opening statement."

Marteen smiled, as if he'd known his for-the-media remarks wouldn't get very far.

"Of course not, Your Honor." His expression became sober as he turned toward the first row on the prosecution's side — and contemptuous as it settled on his prey. "Let's get right to it, then. The defense calls Meg Gallagher."

The camera immediately zoomed in on the stunned reaction.

Meg shook her head, mouthed no. Caroline, recovering more quickly, spoke unseen words to her sister.

Jeffrey was on his feet.

"I'd like to know, before Ms. Gallagher takes the stand, the basis on which the defense believes she's a relevant witness."

"That's fair," Judge Owens replied. "Mr. Marteen?"

"She's *the* relevant witness, Your Honor. I'll admit I'd planned to call another witness first, to lay the groundwork for our interest in her testimony. I thought we'd hear his testimony while Ms. Gallagher was making her way to court. I had no idea she'd be here today. Frankly, we considered her a flight risk, and have had her under surveillance for a while. Our plan was to issue her a summons an hour ago and have a deputy escort her in. I have the subpoena if you'd like it admitted into evidence."

"Let's focus first on the basis on which she's being called."

"The basis, Your Honor, is an observation made by my client the day the trial began. You may recall that Mr. Wynn's opening statement was delayed for several moments because Mr. Beale was whispering to me. We had no way of knowing how significant the observation was until our investigative team looked into it. That's what we've done, Your Honor. And we believe the results of our extensive investigation are significant indeed."

"I take it you'd planned to call your investigator first?"

"Yes, Your Honor. I wasn't going to have him testify to his findings — at least not until we'd heard from Ms. Gallagher. But I was going to have him authenticate the investigative records we will be entering into evidence."

"Tell me a little about the techniques your investigator used."

Marteen gave a knowing smile. "All legal, Your Honor. And no court orders involved. A combination of routine surveillance and retrieval of data available to anyone with access to a telephone or the Internet."

"No phone taps."

"None. And no electronic eavesdropping."

Having asked the questions she would've asked the investigator — to assure herself that whatever the defense had against Meg Gallagher had been legally obtained — Judge Owens spoke to Jeffrey.

"I'm satisfied that Mr. Marteen has a basis for calling this witness." Then she addressed Meg. "Ms. Gallagher? Will you please take the stand?"

No, no, no. Every cell in her body trembled. Her mind whirled. She tried to cling to what Caroline had just said to her. Marteen was grasping at straws. Bringing up her role in preparing the houseboat for market as if that was somehow new.

They probably had found something new, Caroline had whispered during the judge's questions to Marteen. Her fingerprints, most likely. There'd been myriad prints in the houseboat. But, since murder by intruder wasn't anyone's theory of what had happened to Susannah, no attempts at identification had been made. The prints belonged to Kevin's many friends — and possibly, there were leftover prints of Meg's. He'd spent the summer planning a murder, not cleaning house.

Caroline was right. That was it. That was all.

All it *could* be.

So why was she trembling as she made her way to the witness chair?

Because, she told herself, it's natural to feel anxious. It wasn't every day you had a killer staring at you as if he owned you, and his snakelike attorney smiling at you as if you were the best of friends.

They made her angry. Both of them. And that, she discovered, was good.

That made her calm.

"Good morning, Ms. Gallagher."

His voice was pleasant. So was hers.

"Good morning, Mr. Marteen."

"Have you and I ever spoken before?"

"I don't believe so."

"But you and Kevin have."

"No."

"You're saying you don't know my client?"

"I know *of* him."

"But you're not personally acquainted."

"No."

"You've never met."

"Not as far as I know."

"Not as far as you know. Is there some reason you *wouldn't* know?"

Meg had no idea where Marteen believed he was going, but she'd seen enough of his cross-examination of prosecution witnesses to recognize his approach. He was trying to trap her in a lie.

He can't, she reminded herself. There's nothing for me to lie *about.*

"Well," she answered easily, "we're both from Seattle. He's a few years older than I am, and we attended different schools. But it's possible that, at some point, we were at the same place at the same time. If so, I don't remember."

"Let's talk about the past year. You haven't spoken with him, spent time with him?"

"No. I haven't. I —"

"Yes, Ms. Gallagher? Are you remembering something?"

"No." There was nothing to remember. But she was ready to get to her only connection with Kevin Beale — and, more importantly, to get off the stand. "I was just going to say that, as you know, I'm familiar with the houseboat he purchased last summer."

"You're right. I do know. But let's put it on the record. How is it that you happen to be familiar with Kevin's houseboat?"

"I have a small business. I decorate houses that are up for sale."

"To make them look more appealing?"

"To show the home in its best light."

"And one of those homes was Kevin's houseboat?"

"Yes. I decorated it before it went on the market — before the defendant, or any other potential buyer, saw it."

"So you spent time there."

"Of course." Meg heard her own annoyance, and was further annoyed — with herself — for letting it show. She had nothing to hide, but he was making her feel like a criminal . . . and, by letting him provoke her, she was allowing him to win.

"How much time, and how often?"

Meg forced pleasantness back into her voice. "I'd have to check my records. My guess would be that I was inside the houseboat on four or five occasions, for a total of eight hours or so."

"When was your decorating completed?"

"Again I'd have to check. And I'd be delighted to." She smiled. "Offhand, I'd say late April, early May."

"And how many times have you been to Kevin's houseboat since?"

"None."

"None?"

"None."

"You haven't been to Kevin's houseboat since he's lived there?"

"That's right. I haven't been."

"That's your sworn testimony?"

"Yes."

"Your Honor." Jeffrey had risen to his feet.

"Mr. Wynn?"

"I'm sorry to object, but if all of this is simply leading up to the fact that prints in the defendant's houseboat belonged to Ms. Gallagher . . ."

"Mr. Marteen?"

"That's not where this is leading, Your Honor."

"Then proceed."

"Thank you, Your Honor. Let's back up a moment, Ms. Gallagher." Marteen turned to a colleague positioned beside the slide projector. "I'm not as adept with the remote as Mr. Wynn. May I have the first slide, please?"

When the photograph appeared on the screen, he posed a question to Meg. "Do you recognize this car?"

Meg fought a rush of outrage at the intrusion into her privacy.

"Yes. It's mine."

"How long have you owned it?"

"Three years."

"The color's quite distinctive, isn't it?"

"Yes."

"What color is that? Metallic — electric? — blue?"

"I don't know what it's called. The previous owner had it painted, didn't like it and was willing to sell it at a reasonable price."

"But you liked it."

"I liked the cargo space."

"Room for lots of pillows?"

"Yes."

"All right. Next slide. What about this car, Ms. Gallagher? Any idea who owns it?"

"Given the vanity plate, I'd guess it belongs to your client. The defendant."

"Touché, Ms. Gallagher. So, even if you didn't know what Kevin's car looked like — but did know where he lived — you could go to the parking lot near his houseboat and be pretty certain which car was his?"

Where was he going with this? Trying to rattle you, Meg told herself. Snake that he is. Don't let him.

"I imagine so."

"Thank you. By the way, do you remember when you first learned who'd bought the houseboat?"

"I'm not sure of the date."

"But you do remember learning the buyer's name."

"Yes. The listing agent, Anna Casey, told me."

"If Ms. Casey says she has a clear memory of telling you on June fourteenth, an hour or so after the purchase transaction was complete, would you have any reason to doubt it?"

"No. If that's when Anna says she told me, I'm sure it's right."

"Good. Your sister's married to Mr. Wynn, is that correct?"

"Yes."

"How would you describe your relationship with Mrs. Wynn?"

I love her. I'm so proud of her. And these past few months with Caroline have been —

"Ms. Gallagher? Would it be accurate to say that you and your sister are very close?"

Accurate? Very? Meg's eyes darted from Marteen to Caroline. Who was looking worried. But supportive.

"Let's try another approach," Marteen

said. "If I told you we have copies of your cell phone records since the trial began — legally obtained, Your Honor, from an Internet data broker — would it surprise you to hear that you and your sister have spoken almost every day?"

More invasions of privacy. More outrage. And more determination not to let it show.

"No, it wouldn't," she replied.

"And that, on some days, you've spoken multiple times? Ms. Gallagher, would that come as a surprise?"

"No."

"How about phone calls to Mr. Wynn's direct line in his office? Have you made any of those?"

"Yes."

"And when have those calls typically occurred?"

"Early evening."

"After court?"

"Yes."

"Would it be fair to say you and your sister have talked about the trial?"

"Yes."

"And you and your brother-in-law?"

"Yes."

"By the way —" Marteen's voice was silky smooth "— since Kevin's lived in his house-boat, have you driven your car to the parking lot near the gated entrance to the pier?"

The change of direction puzzled her at first. As it was intended to do. But Meg had made a study of the defense counsel, and had discussed with Jeffrey his various tricks. This was one of them, a seemingly out-of-the-blue question meant to catch a witness off guard — and provide an unguarded reply.

The technique wasn't unique to Marteen, Jeffrey had told her. It was a standard trial tactic. She'd seen him using it, too, when he cross-examined witnesses the defense team called.

Meg's reply was the same no matter how the question was posed.

She gave it calmly and confidently. "No."

"What about standing on the dock outside his houseboat?"

"No!"

"You weren't there, on the dock, at any time between 1 a.m. and dawn on Sunday, the fifteenth of August? A few hours after Kevin asked Susannah to be his wife?"

"No!"

"Mr. Marteen," Judge Owens said. "I'm hearing a lot of answers that are making me wonder what we're doing here."

"Ms. Gallagher's answers would make me wonder that, too, Your Honor. But if the

Court will indulge just a few more questions . . ."

"Only a few, Mr. Marteen."

"Thank you, Your Honor." The eyes that returned to Meg had lost all pretense of civility. "Yes or no, Ms. Gallagher. At any time in the past year have you spoken to Kevin Beale?"

"To the best of my knowledge, I have not."

"I'll make it easier for you. Yes or no, at any time on the evening of June twenty-sixth did you and Kevin speak?"

"June twenty-sixth?" *Oh, no. No.*

"Yes or no, Ms. Gallagher."

"I . . . don't know."

"Let's see if this jogs your memory. Next slide."

CHAPTER
TWENTY-THREE

The screen filled with an image — of her. The gallery gasped.

Meg saw a fury in Jeffrey's eyes she felt certain Caroline had never seen . . . and prayed Caroline never would. And, on her sister's face, Meg saw sadness — and support.

"Is this you, Ms. Gallagher?"

Meg returned her gaze to the inquisitor who'd trapped her after all. His smugness was preferable, less painful than Jeffrey's anger and Caroline's dismay.

"Yes."

"Dancing."

"Yes."

"Smiling."

"Yes."

"Will you please identify the man with whom you're dancing and smiling?"

"The defendant."

"Let's hear his name, Ms. Gallagher."

"Kevin Beale."

"Will you tell Judge Owens where this photograph was taken?"

"In the Rainier Room at the Wind Chimes Hotel."

"On what occasion?"

"It was a wedding reception."

"Were you Kevin's date, or did you meet him there?"

"I wasn't his date! And . . ."

"And?"

"I don't remember meeting him, or dancing with him."

"I beg your pardon?"

"I don't *remember.*"

"Are you saying this photograph is a fake? If so, we have a number of others — could we set them to run automatically? — taken on more than one cell phone by more than one wedding guest who recognized Kevin, and fortunately for us, didn't delete the pictures they took. Are you saying it's a fake? That the defense is perpetrating a fraud on this Court?"

"No."

"Good. So you do remember."

"*No.* I don't." She should have looked at Caroline and Jeffrey as she confessed. But she couldn't force herself to do it. Instead, she recalled Caroline's loving words from yesterday afternoon. *You're not an outsider. You're our family. And,* she'd added proudly, *you're Jeffrey's secret weapon . . .* who, Meg realized as she met Marteen's arrogant eyes, had just sabotaged Jeffrey's case. "I had a lot to drink that night. Too much to drink."

"That's really convenient, isn't it?"

"It's the *truth,* Mr. Marteen. I don't remember meeting him. Seeing these photographs doesn't *make* me remember."

"Isn't the truth, Ms. Gallagher, that you found yourself extremely attracted to Mr. Beale?"

"No!"

"No, you didn't, or no, you don't remember?"

"Both."

"You don't remember meeting him, but you remember *not* being attracted to him? How does that work?"

"I *know* I wouldn't have been attracted to him."

"No matter how intoxicated you happened to be?"

"Yes."

"Hold on a minute," Judge Owens said. "Let me just recap where we are. Ms. Gallagher is familiar with the location of Mr. Beale's houseboat. That's something we already knew. In the past couple of months

252

she's spoken with some frequency to her sister and brother-in-law. Not surprisingly, they've discussed the trial the entire city is talking about. The defense investigation has uncovered photographs of Ms. Gallagher dancing with Mr. Beale at a wedding reception two months prior to Susannah Nichols's death. I'm assuming that Mr. Beale's memory of that encounter resulted from his seeing Ms. Gallagher during opening statements?"

"Yes, Your Honor," Marteen replied. "He'd known the woman he'd met at the reception only as Meg. She didn't tell him her last name, or of her relationship to the houseboat he'd recently purchased. That connection, as well as her relationship to Mr. Wynn, came as a complete shock to my client on the first day of the trial."

"Okay. So now we know that Ms. Gallagher and Mr. Beale shared a few dances. We also know that Ms. Gallagher has sworn under oath that she has no memory of those dances. Since she doesn't remember meeting Mr. Beale, she couldn't be expected to disclose their meeting to either her sister or brother-in-law. Am I missing something, Mr. Marteen?"

"No, Your Honor. And, I have to admit, it hadn't occurred to me that Ms. Gallagher would claim amnesia. I thought we'd have a case of *he said, she said,* not a *he said, she says she can't remember.* We have the photographs, however, and witnesses who are prepared to testify that the photographs are an accurate reflection of what they saw. My guess would be that, like Mr. Beale himself, none of these witnesses had any reason to suspect Ms. Gallagher was as intoxicated as she's now claiming to have been."

"Again, Mr. Marteen, where is the relevance to this trial?"

"It's in what took place *after* these photographs, Your Honor, beginning with a conversation between Kevin and Ms. Gallagher when the band took a break . . . and continuing for the next seven weeks. I have a feeling Ms. Gallagher is going to plead no memory of that conversation."

"Is this correct, Ms. Gallagher?" the judge asked.

"Yes," Meg admitted. "I remember arriving at the reception and listening to the band. I have no memory of dancing, or of any conversation I might've had."

"All right," Judge Owens said. "I'm going to permit Mr. Marteen to tell me what he believes I need to know. Ms. Gallagher will remain in the witness chair, since I gather much of what Mr. Marteen has to say involves her. Mr. Marteen?"

It was a gift. A defense attorney's dream. Even a polished litigator like Greg Marteen needed a moment to recover from the shock.

"The date of the wedding reception is important, Your Honor. It was the night following the Friday-afternoon phone call informing Mr. Beale that he was one of the remaining candidates for the network job — and questions about his unborn child were raised. As you recall, Your Honor, first thing Monday morning, Mr. Beale told the network of his intention to marry Ms. Nichols. He'd told Ms. Gallagher of that decision thirty-six hours earlier, during the band break Saturday night. She wasn't shy about her interest in him, or subdued in her reaction when he told her no. She's a very beautiful woman. She's not accustomed to being rejected. She became angry. Enraged. Her fury surprised Kevin, as did the off-color language she used. But he extricated himself from the situation, and — until he saw her again during opening statements — didn't give it another thought . . . even though he should have."

Marteen paused.

"I'm not going to ask any questions," Judge Owens said, "until you're through."

Marteen nodded. "On a number of occasions during the seven weeks leading up to Susannah's death, he saw what we now know is Ms. Gallagher's distinctive blue SUV. He assumed it belonged to a houseboat owner on a nearby pier. When he spotted it outside his bank, or at a restaurant where he'd been dining with friends, or a few cars behind him in traffic, he concluded that he and the unknown neighbor had similar destinations."

Marteen's shrug underscored how untroubled his client had been.

"He wasn't on the lookout for a stalker. If he'd realized he was being followed by the woman who'd been so incensed when he rebuffed her sexual overtures at the reception, he'd have told her to stop. But he wouldn't have been particularly concerned. So she knew where he lived. It wasn't a secret. And short of approaching by water, he figured the parking lot was as close to the houseboat as she'd get.

"What Kevin didn't know, until opening statements, was that the woman who'd been angered by his rejection *did* have access to his houseboat — and to the dock where Susannah was standing when she left Kevin's bed, around 1:00 a.m., to make a phone call.

"Access to the pier's locked gate is by

code or by key. Ms. Gallagher was given the code used by the previous owner when she was hired to spruce up the houseboat with her pillows. She was also given a key to the houseboat itself. She returned the key, and we have no evidence — nor do we suggest — that she made a copy before returning it. Kevin didn't re-key the houseboat. Most new homeowners don't. Nor did he change the four-digit entry code to the gate."

Marteen's expression, as he looked at his client, was clear. What he meant to convey was that Kevin Beale might be a celebrity, but he was just like everyone else.

"We don't know where Ms. Gallagher was between 1:00 a.m. and dawn the night Susannah Nichols died. It's a question I intend to ask her. We do know where she *wasn't*. In one of those tragic ironies, and as published in a newspaper article last November, Caroline Wynn miscarried the couple's baby at approximately the same time Susannah and her unborn baby died. Mr. and Mrs. Wynn were at Queen Anne Medical Center. Ms. Gallagher wasn't at her sister's bedside."

This time, the defense counsel's expression begged the obvious question: Why *wasn't* Meg with her sister in Caroline's hour of need? Marteen proceeded to give the jury the answer.

"Kevin's engagement to Susannah was announced on local television newscasts at ten and eleven. Radio had it on their top-of-the-hour news updates throughout the night. From the surveillance we've conducted on Ms. Gallagher, we've observed that, based on when she turns off her inside lights, her usual bedtime is midnight. She lives alone and isn't dating. Her phone records tell us that, with the exception of Jeffrey and Caroline Wynn, her calls are business-related. We've been unable to retrieve phone records from last summer, and have no way of conducting retrospective surveillance. But if she was as obsessed with Kevin Beale as we believe she may have been, it's possible that, on hearing the news of his engagement, she drove to his home. After unlocking the gate, using the four-digit code she'd used in the recent past, she walked onto the pier. For all we know, she'd spent many nights on the dock outside his houseboat. Standing vigil, if you will. That might have been her intent that night. But there was Susannah, wearing Kevin's football jersey —"

"I get the picture," the judge intervened. "Any other *factual* bits of information I need to know?"

"Ms. Gallagher is tall. Long boned. Her

hands, though slender, are large. She used to teach aerobics, and, from our observations, maintains a rigorous exercise regime. She runs. *And she swims.* It's our contention, Your Honor, that Meg Gallagher may have happened upon Susannah Nichols and reacted with the same kind of rage witnessed by Kevin on the night he rejected her. We further contend that this troubled woman would have confessed her crime of passion to her two closest friends, perhaps her *only* friends. The lead prosecutor and his wife."

CHAPTER
TWENTY-FOUR

Marteen fell silent.

Judge Owens looked concerned.

The camera zoomed in, once again, on Meg.

She was slumped in the witness chair, a sinking that had progressively deepened with each devastating insinuation the defense attorney had made. Her head was bent, her eyes focused on the fingers Marteen had just implied were capable of holding a pregnant woman under water until she died.

The camera watched as Judge Owens turned to Meg.

"These are very serious allegations."

Meg heard the words vaguely, as if spoken from afar. It was she who was under water, forced down, held down, unable to move . . . or to breathe. Her brain was screaming for oxygen — even as it knew all was lost. The knowledge was achingly clear. There'd be a mistrial. Judge Owens had no choice. Jeffrey's reputation would be destroyed, or worse. Meg probably, ultimately, wouldn't be charged with the crime she hadn't committed. But her possible role in Susannah's death would be out there, for Marteen to raise again and again should Kevin be retried — which he almost certainly wouldn't be. The next prosecutor would know it was a case he couldn't win. There'd always be reasonable doubt because of her.

The killer would go free.

Susannah's struggle as she was held under water had been in vain. Her brain had screamed for oxygen, too — even as it had realized, as Meg was realizing, that all was lost.

No.

In that instant Meg Gallagher did what Susannah Nichols could not.

She surfaced. With the grace of the ballerina she'd once been. Shoulders squared. Head high. She rested her hands on the railing in front of her, the long slender fingers that would never hurt another living thing, as she addressed the judge.

"Vicious allegations, Your Honor. And false ones."

"It's my responsibility to advise you to say nothing further," Judge Owens said, "until you've had the opportunity to discuss the situation with an attorney. I see that your brother-in-law is standing. I suspect he was going to offer the same advice."

"I was, Your Honor," Jeffrey said.

Meg met Jeffrey's gaze, saw resignation where fury had been. Then she made herself look at her sister. She saw determined support — and extreme pallor. Meg was standing, moving, as she exclaimed, *"Caroline!"*

Jeffrey reached Caroline first. He was crouching in front of her, touching her, when Meg arrived.

"I'm fine," Caroline insisted, and had been insisting, since Meg's alarmed outburst.

"You don't *look* fine," Meg said.

"You need to lie down," Jeffrey added. "And I want to call Kathleen."

"I'm *fine.*" Caroline's assertion was accompanied by a transformation as dramatic as what court watchers had just observed in her sister on the witness stand — as if Caroline, too, had been drowning . . . and found the strength, or the will, to break free.

There was no disputing how much better she looked, and no arguing with her, either.

"Really." She raised her hand, and a grateful, embarrassed smile curved the cheeks

that had gone from ashen to rosy. "Go away!"

Meg and Jeffrey remained where they were, hovering instead of crouching, and turned toward the judge when she spoke.

"I was about to suggest that I adjourn the hearing."

"No." Meg took a few steps forward. "I don't need an attorney, Your Honor. I didn't stalk the defendant. I didn't go to his houseboat. I had *nothing* to do with Susannah and Matthew's murder. I'd like to answer any questions Mr. Marteen — or you — must have for me. I understand my legal rights. I believe I also have the right to be heard."

"Meg." Jeffrey had moved a few steps forward, too. His voice was hushed, but his legal counsel was clear.

Meg replied quietly, "This is my decision, Jeffrey." To the judge, she said, "This is what I want to do."

Judge Owens nodded, then angled her head toward Caroline. "Why don't we take a thirty-minute recess before the questioning begins?"

Caroline's answer was to leap to her feet as energetically as, at the onset of the hearing, the defense had done. "Not on my account, Your Honor."

"Ms. Gallagher?"

"I'm ready to answer Mr. Marteen's questions."

Judge Owens gestured toward the witness chair and reminded her that she was still under oath.

Once Meg was seated, Marteen approached.

"I believe I know your answer to my first question, but allow me to ask it anyway. Did you make sexual overtures to Mr. Beale?"

"No."

"Do you remember not doing it?"

"No."

"Let me guess, it's something you'd never do?"

"That's right."

"Did you stalk Kevin Beale?"

"No."

"Do you remember not stalking him, or do you suffer from alcohol-related amnesia on a daily basis?"

"One moment, please, Ms. Gallagher." Judge Owens held up her hand. "I'm speaking now to the legal pundits who are going to have a field day with the unorthodox nature of this hearing. Mr. Marteen's question is argumentative. I know that. Mr. Wynn knows that. Mr. Marteen knows that. Mr. Wynn is respecting my request to withhold objections, and Mr. Marteen knows that he's already gotten exceptional leniency in his manner of questioning and in presenting his case. The party's over. I want to hear testimony that's pertinent to the reason we're here. With regard to Ms. Gallagher, that means her whereabouts on the night Susannah and Matthew Nichols died."

Judge Owens spoke to Meg. "You don't have to answer the last question. Unless you want to."

"I do want to, Your Honor. I remember *not* stalking the defendant. And I never drink and drive."

After registering surprise, Marteen said, "To the night in question, then. We know where you weren't, at the hospital with your sister. That's correct, isn't it?"

"Yes." Caroline hadn't called her, wouldn't have called her. *Then.* They weren't sisters then. Meg hadn't learned about the miscarriage until Caroline could talk about it — many days later.

"Where were you that night, Ms. Gallagher? If you remember."

"I remember."

"Then tell us."

"I was working."

"Sewing pillows in your home?"

"Arranging pillows in the homes I'd sewn them for."

"At night?"

"Yes. I left my place at ten or so, and returned the following morning around eight. I went to three houses. They all needed to be ready for Sunday afternoon."

"Was anyone with you?"

"No."

"Yes or no, for the past two months you've been in bed by midnight."

"Yes, but —"

"But last August fourteenth you spent all night working?"

"Yes."

"Yes or no, have you pulled a similar all-nighter — even once — during the past two months?"

"No."

"So that was pretty unusual."

"No."

"I'd like a little narrative here," Judge Owens said. "Ms. Gallagher, please explain."

"My usual pattern is, or at least *has been,* to do much of the final arranging late at night. Mr. Marteen's surveillance team hasn't documented that pattern because for the past two months I haven't taken on any new work."

"Why not?" the judge asked.

"I wanted to watch the trial." Meg paused. "And to be available for my sister."

"Thank you," Judge Owens replied. "Please continue, Mr. Marteen."

"Do you remember where the houses were?"

"Of course. I have the addresses at home, and the names of the real estate agents who requested that I complete the work by Sunday. All three were on the eastside. The first two were on the Sammamish plateau. The third was in Carnation."

"You were alone." Marteen emphasized it again.

"Yes."

"Any way you can prove you were there?"

"The houses were ready for showing when they needed to be."

"Which was when?"

"From one until four Sunday afternoon."

"So, they would've been ready if you'd left Kevin's houseboat at 2:00 a.m. and returned home around noon?"

"I *wasn't* at the defendant's houseboat."

"Did you see Susannah standing alone on the dock?"

"No!"

"Did you sneak up behind her and shove

her toward the hull of the speedboat?"

"No, Mr. Marteen, I did not."

"Did you hold her under water till she and her unborn baby drowned?"

"That's what *your* client did, Mr. Marteen."

"Where's the proof you weren't there, Ms. Gallagher?"

"Where's the proof that I was?"

"That's not an answer." He frowned. "Yes or no, can you prove you weren't at Mr. Beale's houseboat the night Susannah died?"

"Give me a lie detector test. Right here. Right now."

Marteen's smirk was followed by his dismissive shrug. Coldly, he repeated, "Yes or no, can you prove you weren't at Mr. Beale's the night Susannah died? Yes. Or no."

"No."

"I have no more questions for this witness, Your Honor." Marteen's smirk returned, for the camera, as he walked to his chair beside his client.

Jeffrey, standing, waited until Marteen was seated before he addressed the bench.

"I'm planning to question Ms. Gallagher, Your Honor. But I wonder if I could have a few moments?"

"A thirty-minute recess?"

"A thirty-minute recess would be good."

CHAPTER
TWENTY-FIVE

Caroline, Jeffrey and Meg went alone to the prosecution conference area that was a private corridor away from the courtroom itself.

The other members of Jeffrey's team, with whom Meg had nibbled on pizza as they'd all tried to guess what Marteen had up his sleeve, could have joined them. But they, too, had seen Jeffrey's fury. And stayed away.

"I'm so sorry," Meg said.

"It's not your fault," Caroline replied as she sat down at the table in the center of the room. Neither Jeffrey nor Meg followed her lead.

"Yes, Caroline, it is. If I'd remembered meeting Kevin Beale, I would've told you and Jeffrey, and it would've been disclosed, and regarded as the no big deal it was, and —"

"There isn't any point in talking about it," Jeffrey interjected. "That's not what happened. Not where we are."

"Where are we?" Meg asked.

Jeffrey didn't mince words. "In trouble."

"You're saying Judge Owens didn't believe Meg's testimony?" Caroline asked incredulously.

"I'm sure she did believe it," Jeffrey told her.

"But it doesn't matter," Meg said. "What she believes doesn't matter. I *know* lie detector results aren't admissible in a court of law. But doing the actual exam in the courtroom, on television . . ."

Jeffrey had begun shaking his head long before she stopped speaking. "No."

"What about sodium pentothal? I'm serious, Jeffrey. I'll do anything you can think of."

"What I need, I'm afraid, is the one thing you can't give me — irrefutable evidence that you were miles away from Lake Union at the time Susannah died."

"I can't give you that, Jeffrey. I'm so sorry."

"I know you are, Meg."

Silence fell briefly before a voice spoke from the open doorway behind them.

"Meg may not believe she can provide the proof you need," the trauma surgeon said, "but I'm pretty certain she can."

"Mark," Meg whispered as she turned. Mark, and the prosecution-team member who'd escorted him to the secluded room. "What — ?"

"Am I doing here?" He smiled. "Helping, I hope."

"I don't have proof."

"I think you do. Or someone does," he clarified to Jeffrey. "Will the judge let you put me on the stand?"

Jeffrey nodded. "Given what she's permitted the defense to do, and how she's probably regretting it, I think that'll be a request she's happy to grant."

"Wouldn't we have gotten to this point anyway?" Caroline asked. "Marteen's insinuation that Meg was somehow involved?"

"Sure," Jeffrey acknowledged. "And I have to admire Judge Owens for cutting to the chase. I have a feeling she assumed that wherever Marteen was heading would be easier to deal with than it is."

"Maybe it'll become easy," Mark said. "Ask me about the reception, Jeffrey, if the judge will let you."

"Okay."

"I don't have much to say about the stalking allegation, except there's no way in hell that's something Meg would do."

"If I can," Jeffrey said, "I'll work out a

way for you to say that. Otherwise I'll skip to the night Susannah died."

"Good," Mark agreed as Jeffrey glanced at his watch, signaling that the recess was nearing an end.

"Mark . . ."

He met her worried eyes. "I'd fall on a sword for you, Meg. If I had to. In this instance, I don't. I'm going to tell the truth, just like you did."

Judge Owens returned late, and a little breathless, from the recess. She had a stack of avocado-green telephone message slips in her hand.

Without explanation, she placed them beside her and called the hearing to order.

"You're on, Mr. Wynn."

"Thank you, Your Honor. I'd like to postpone my examination of Ms. Gallagher and call Dr. Mark Traynor to the stand."

Marteen shifted noisily in his chair, but didn't have the nerve to object.

After Mark was sworn in, Jeffrey asked a few identifying questions.

"You're a trauma surgeon at Queen Anne Medical Center?"

"I am."

"And, for the viewers to whom you look familiar, you've appeared on television from time to time?"

"Yes. In situations in which the patient or patient's family have granted permission to discuss aspects of treatment with the press."

"Will you please tell the court why you're here this morning?"

"I left work just as the hearing began. I listened on the car radio. I was about halfway home when I turned around and drove here. It occurred to me that I had information Meg wasn't able to provide."

"You referred to Ms. Gallagher as Meg."

"We met a year ago January, and dated until mid-April."

"Of last year."

"Yes. We were together for three months."

"And since then?"

"We've seen each other twice. Let me clarify that. *I've* seen Meg twice. She's only seen me — remembers seeing me — once. The time she remembers was five months ago. That's when we both learned that she had no memory of seeing me at the wedding reception in the Rainier Room."

"Did she tell you why she had no memory of seeing you?"

"She'd had a lot to drink."

"Were you aware of it at the time?"

"Not really. Her motor skills were good. She danced beautifully. But she seemed . . .

unfocused. In her own private world."

"While she was dancing?"

"Yes. I haven't seen the photographs Mr. Marteen presented. But I'm fully prepared to believe that those pictures could've been taken in a way that made it appear Meg was dancing with the defendant — or, for that matter, with any of a number of men. There was more group dancing than couples' dancing. Anyone who felt like dancing did."

"You're saying Meg wasn't dancing specifically with the defendant."

"That's what I'm saying. I feel sure there are other wedding guests who'd say the same thing. The defendant and I arrived at the reception an hour or so into it and, as it happens, at the same time. I don't recall Mr. Marteen mentioning that Mr. Beale was an uninvited guest — uninvited, at any rate, by the bride or groom. I overheard his conversation with two guests, two women, who ran into him in the lobby and invited him to join the party."

"Do you know what he was doing at the hotel?"

"No idea."

"Did the invited wedding guests know who he was?"

"My guess would be yes. They didn't call him by name, but it was clear they regarded him as . . . special."

"Did *you* know who he was?"

"Not then. At some point during the pretrial publicity, I realized that's who he must have been. I felt grateful that Meg had interacted with him only in passing, left the reception shortly after he arrived and got home safely."

"Tell us about the interaction."

"He tried to talk to her, the way other men were trying. I can't tell you if she even heard what he, or anyone, said. The music was playing, she was dancing. Her response to any man getting close enough to attempt what would've been a shouted conversation was to dance away from him."

"Including the defendant."

"Including the defendant."

"And when the band took a break?"

"Meg had hired a town car for the evening. As she testified, she never drinks and drives. She must have told the driver to find her in the Rainier Room at a specified time. He was standing at the edge of the dance floor when the band announced its break. The defendant followed Meg off the dance floor, at one point attempting to stop her by reaching for her arm. The touch startled her. But she smiled, shook it off — shook him off — and moments later left the reception with the driver."

"You didn't see Meg make a pass at the defendant."

"She *didn't* make a pass at him. The opposite happened."

"Did the defendant appear upset at being rebuffed?"

"No. Just as Meg didn't seem upset when he touched her arm."

"Is it possible there was a conversation between Meg and Mr. Beale that you missed?"

"No."

"Why not?"

"Meg's the reason I went to the reception. I never took my eyes off her. And," Mark said softly, "when she left, I followed her home. I was worried about her. As I've said, she seemed lost in her own private world. A sad world, I thought, even though she smiled as she danced."

"Did you talk to her that night?"

"No. I certainly considered it. I wanted to. In the end, I decided she'd spent the evening escaping from men who were trying to impose what they wanted on her. She didn't need another one. I made sure she got home safely. Then I left."

Mark cast a glance at Greg Marteen. "If there's a stalker in the courtroom today, it's me, Mr. Marteen, not Meg."

The moment lingered until, Mark's point eloquently made, Jeffrey spoke again to his witness.

"You don't believe Meg stalked the defendant."

"Not a chance."

"You sound very definite, Dr. Traynor," the judge observed. "I'd like to know why."

"She's not that confident." Mark looked at the judge. But he was speaking to Meg. "It takes a fair amount of ego to force yourself on someone who's rejected you. She wouldn't put herself in that position — of being rejected — to begin with. She'd never make the first move toward a man, much less a blatant sexual overture. And, for the record, she doesn't swear. Truth be told, she's a bit of a prude. She's so uncertain of herself, of her worth, she even runs away from the people who love her."

"I see."

It was obvious that Judge Owens did see what Mark Traynor was saying — and how the handsome trauma surgeon felt.

"Meg has expressed uncertainty about being able to prove her whereabouts on the night of Susannah Nichols's death," Jeffrey said. "Is that a reflection of her lack of confidence?"

"No." Mark smiled. "I think we can credit that to Mr. Marteen. He was accusing her of the unimaginable. It's not surprising she couldn't remember the mundane. It's also possible she doesn't realize the trail of proof she created."

"Please explain."

"Most of the homes Meg works in have lockboxes. The house key's inside the box, which is opened using a personal code. Every real estate agent has the code. And because of her role in the marketing process, so does Meg. Whenever a given code is entered, a record is made of the time, date, address and user name. I'm not sure Meg knows the extent of the record that's generated whenever the lockbox is opened. We didn't discuss it when we were together, and I only learned about it from an article — on security issues for agents — I read a number of months ago."

Mark looked beyond Jeffrey to Meg. He wasn't the only one looking at her. Indeed, with the exception of the defense, everyone was.

And they saw what he did. She *hadn't* known.

Mark's eyes held hers as he continued.

"If there were lockboxes on the homes Meg visited that night —" her head nodded as she mouthed *There were* "— there'll be a record of when she entered each one."

Mark didn't want to withdraw his gaze from Meg. But he had a feeling the defense attorney who'd treated Meg so badly was still gloating from the victory he believed he'd won.

Mark was going to set Kevin Beale's lawyer straight. He faced him as he spoke. "I know what Mr. Marteen is thinking. So what? She logs in, tosses a few pillows here and there, makes a detour to the houseboat before logging in to the next home on her list."

"You're suggesting there's additional proof?" Jeffrey asked.

"There's not a doubt in my mind. And, like the lockbox recordings, Meg's oblivious to it. She becomes absorbed in what she's doing, so intent on her work she forgets how exposed she is. As she told Mr. Marteen, her usual pattern is to work late at night. Alone, in an empty house, with the lights on and making trips back and forth to her car."

"You're saying someone will have seen her that night."

"I'd bet on it. In those populated neigh-borhoods, on a Saturday night in August, I'd bet on many someones."

"So would I," Jeffrey said softly. "So would I. I have no more questions for Dr. Traynor, Your Honor."

But the defense attorney did.

"You're quite fond of Ms. Gallagher, aren't you?"

"That's putting it mildly, Mr. Marteen. I'm in love with her."

"That's all, Your Honor," Marteen said. "All I need to know."

"Before I excuse Dr. Traynor — with the admonition not to speak with the press, or vice versa, until the end of the trial — I have something that he, as well as the rest of you, might find interesting." Judge Owens picked up the stack of phone messages. "These represent calls received by my office prior to the recess. They're from people like Dr. Traynor who, in listening to this morning's hearing, realize they have a contribution to make. Several are from neighbors who recall seeing Ms. Gallagher putting pillows in the empty homes. . . ."

CHAPTER
TWENTY-SIX

Eleven hours later, Mark opened his door to the woman he loved.

He'd last seen her, in the flesh, when he'd exited the courtroom. He'd seen her image on TV on the evening news — close-ups of the testimony which, by the time the hearing was adjourned, had been shown to be true.

Marteen's backpedaling, too, had made the news. His client and Ms. Gallagher's *lover* merely had differing memories of what had happened at the reception. And, Marteen insisted, Kevin Beale *had* seen an SUV resembling Ms. Gallagher's SUV on numerous occasions. But, Marteen conceded, it may have been merely a resemblance, another automobile with a colorful coat of paint.

And, as to the suggestion that Meg Gallagher was involved in Susannah's death, the defense had been obliged to follow the various coincidences wherever they led. Marteen proclaimed that he was *glad* the prosecutor's sister-in-law — and Jeffrey himself — had been vindicated of all wrongdoing.

He went on to say this meant Susannah's death had been the accident the defense had always contended — and which they'd prove, beyond all doubt, when it was their turn to present evidence. As tragic as such a death was, accidental drowning was easier for her loved ones — his client included — to live with than murder at the hands of an obsessed "other woman" would have been.

"Meg," Mark said. "Come in."

"I wanted to thank you."

"I was just the first in a line of witnesses for the prosecution who told the whole truth and nothing but the truth."

"Well. I appreciate it."

"You're welcome. You could have called to tell me that."

"I could have," she answered. Then shook her head.

"You couldn't have?"

"Not really."

"Because there's something else?"

"Because," Meg whispered, "there's everything else."

■ ■ ■ ■

They talked, and touched. Touching while they talked.

They made love, and talked again when they were entwined so closely there was no room for lies.

"Caroline's pregnant," Mark said.

"Yes, she is."

"And you're not."

"No. Well, I could be."

"Oh?" Mark kissed what he knew, even in darkness, would be a frown of uncertainty on her brow. "Would that be a recent development?"

"Very recent. The baby —"

"Our baby."

"— would be only a few minutes old. Would that be okay — if I'm pregnant, I mean?"

"What do you think?" he asked. His kisses were gentle, and purposeful. He'd kiss, and keep kissing, until every wrinkle of uncertainty melted away.

He felt it happening, beneath his lips, and in the body joined with his.

"I think it would be."

She could feel him smile. "I *know* it would. More than okay."

"Far more," Meg whispered. "And safe. I haven't had anything to drink since the night I saw you on the terrace."

"Has that been difficult?"

"At times."

"When the emotions have gotten tough?"

Meg started to nod. Then stopped. "But not today, Mark. Not today. Even when I could see how angry Jeffrey was, and how sad Marteen's accusations were making my sister, I didn't want to run from the courtroom and find the nearest liquor store."

"What did you want?"

"To stay and fight."

"When the emotions get tough," Mark said, "Meg gets tougher."

"I guess so."

"It's more than that, you know. When her loved ones need her, Meg is there. . . ."

An hour later, the chance and hope of a baby later, Mark asked whether she would have returned to their love had it not been for the events of that day.

"I promised myself I'd try. I might have done a little stalking first."

"Not confident stalking."

"No. What you said in court was true. If I'd followed you, watched you, it would've been to see if you'd found someone else, and were so obviously in love with her that I should stay away."

"That would've been my rationale for watching you."

"You heard what Marteen said his surveillance revealed. I wasn't dating anyone. I haven't," she said, "since you."

"Neither have I." Mark felt her surprise. "Why would it be any different for me? I missed you, loved you, had no interest in being with anyone else. Couldn't you tell from the way I've been making love to you?"

"It's felt the same as before, Mark. The way our lovemaking always feels."

"Like coming home."

"Like coming home," she echoed. "Like being home."

CHAPTER
TWENTY-SEVEN

Monday, June 13
7:00 p.m.
Dearest Bobbi,

I need to tell you about today.

I need to write about it myself.

The best way, I suppose, is to describe the events as they happened.

The day began happily, as every day does with you. Court was dark — it's Monday — and, since the defense is presenting its evidence (such as it is), and all your dad has to do is prepare his brilliant cross-exams, he was able to play with us a little longer before leaving for work.

He pretended he was hanging around to talk to me. But who he *really* wanted to talk to was you.

You loved it. You always do.

"Hello, little Bobbi," he says.

And in a flurry of kicks you reply.

You love his voice, don't you? You hear his love.

We puttered after he left, getting ready — in a leisurely way — for this month's visit with Kathleen.

Meg arrived at nine to drive us.

I asked her, right away, about Mark. It's such fun to watch her blush with happiness and to see her joy.

"We're in love," she said — with smiling emphasis on the "we're." It's taken her awhile to say aloud what she's finally accepted to be true. She's so much in love with Mark . . . and he's every bit as much in love with her.

"Really?" I teased. "You and Mark?"

She laughed and asked, "How's Bobbi today?"

"Well rested and dancing. Want to feel?"

She did want to, but her hand hovered until I guided it to where you'd been dancing.

You'd stopped by then.

"Bobbi?" I said. "Say hello to Aunt Meg."

And you did, you nice girl. Aunt Meg! Aunt Meg!

Did you feel her touch? The gentleness and the love?

"She's really active, isn't she? And big."

"*So* big." I gave her your stats. "Two pounds. Twelve inches."

"That's all?"

"That's exactly where she's supposed to be." I told her your eyes were open, and that — as you so thoughtfully demonstrated — you respond to sound. You have fingerprints, too, and toeprints. Yours alone, designed by your DNA and crafted by those merry cells. "As of a week ago, she was old enough to survive on her own."

"Not that she's going to have to."

"Oh, no. She and I are going the distance, the full nine months."

I felt confident when I said that, Bobbi. I had no idea — not the slightest inkling — that a few hours later, during my routine appointment with Kathleen, I'd learn that we probably won't go the full nine months, after all.

But, my darling, I will keep you inside me until it's safe for you to be born.

I will.

Needless to say, the appointment was far from routine. My blood pressure, which has always been nice and low, has become elevated to the minimal level required for the diagnosis — preeclampsia — Kathleen's now given me. I'm "spilling" protein, too.

I couldn't believe it. I've been feeling so healthy, so well (and still do!).

But, Kathleen says, that's how preeclampsia usually happens. Out of the blue. Along about the fifth month. Without a symptom in sight.

It's the reason "routine" prenatal exams are essential.

The preeclampsia's mild at the moment. Mild enough that Kathleen feels comfortable prescribing bed rest at home.

Mild sounded hopeful, Caroline thought. As if they'd caught the preeclampsia in time to cure it. But there was only one "cure," ending the reason for the high blood pressure in the first place — the pregnancy itself.

Mild *was* hopeful, she told herself. And mild was where her preeclampsia would remain for as long as Bobbi needed to stay inside her. Even if, when, it progressed — as Kathleen said it inevitably would — there'd be no cure, no matter how ill Caroline became, until Bobbi could enter the world without struggling to survive . . . without wondering, as she gasped for breath and was stuck with needles, what had become of the cozy sanctuary she'd known.

I'm going to do everything Kathleen tells me I must, and not one thing she says I mustn't.

Both lists are easy.

You and I get to lounge in bed thinking happy thoughts. Except for the lounging, that's our usual day.

I'll check my blood pressure at four- to six-hour intervals — or Meg will, or your dad will, and Meg's already talking about having Mark come by at least once a day. I always love to see him, I told her, but that's *not* going to happen, because it doesn't *need* to happen.

Kathleen's given us an automated blood-pressure cuff. It's the correct size for my arm, is in synch with her office readings, and as long as the instructions are followed, it's fool-proof. We all — your dad included — demonstrated our mastery of the instructions before leaving Kathleen's office.

I'll be checking for urine protein, too, and weighing myself every day.

There are specific signs and symptoms to watch for. But Kathleen wants to hear about *any* symptoms, any changes, whether on the watch list or not, and whenever they occur.

Those are our musts.

Here are the must-nots.

Watch, read, think, do or talk about anything stressful. Stress doesn't cause preeclampsia. But stress increases blood pressure, no matter what its cause, and the goal is to prevent further elevation.

Kathleen was adamant with Meg that the stress of last month's hearing — and Meg's inadvertent role in prompting it — wasn't a factor in where we are today. Neither was the blahness I experienced the day before the hearing, or my episode of looking awful (apparently) while Meg was on the stand. Meg hadn't failed in her promise to put me in the car and rush me to the hospital should a crisis arrive. She hadn't missed any symptoms she should've seen.

Kathleen was equally adamant in identifying Meg's (unwarranted) guilt as a topic she and I weren't to discuss.

Also: no more trial, even though it's going well. (Meg's recording it, for any postpartum viewing you and I might like to do.) Marteen's trying his best to damage the prosecution's case, but — so far — he hasn't made a dent. And he won't. But his attempts may get ugly . . . and that *would* make me mad.

And: no Internet.

And: no reading about preeclampsia. Kathleen will tell me what she wants me to know, and all I need to know. Everything else, the pages and pages of what *can* happen, would be an undue source of worry.

Kathleen asked me to close my copy of Williams's *Obstetrics,* the definitive textbook for physicians, which she knows I have, and keep it closed until after you're born. I agreed, of course. So it wasn't concern that I'd go back on my promise that made Meg commandeer the textbook before leaving me this afternoon.

I was the born reader, Bobbi. And Meg was

the born dancer. I was also the bossy mom.

My sister plans to be the reader now. And, if this afternoon of tucking me in and taking my blood pressure is any indication, Meg's also going to be the — very — bossy mom. She'll look after me with love, the way I once looked after her.

And you know what I'll do, what we'll do? You in my tummy, and I in my bed?

Ma in her kerchief, and I in my cap, Caroline thought as the similarly rhythmic words flowed into her journal. Soothing words. Mementos of a happy time, in bed with her sister, years ago.

We'll dance, little one.
We will dance.

CHAPTER
TWENTY-EIGHT

Thursday, July 28
2:00 p.m.
My dear girl,

We're doing so well, you especially. My pressure's only up a bit over the past six weeks, and I'm symptom-free and feeling fine.

We've made weekly trips to see Kathleen. Easy trips, thanks to Meg. The purpose of these visits isn't for Kathleen to double-check the blood pressure readings — and weights and protein measurements — I've been doing at home.

Those are accurate. We've even had a trauma surgeon involved. He's just "happened to be" in the company of the love of his life when she's making her "daily rounds." We've now shown unequivocally that whether an architect or a doctor presses the button that tells the cuff to inflate automatically and provide its bright red digital readout, the result's the same. It's been great seeing Mark . . . seeing his side of their love.

The weekly checkups are for you. Kathleen hasn't said as much, but the worry Meg can't *quite* hide as Kathleen's doing her in utero measurements of you and Meg's totally *un*-hidden relief when everything's right where it's supposed to be is a pretty clear indicator that preeclampsia can interfere with nutritional supply to the baby . . . but not *our* baby.

You're growing (and dancing), and I'm thinking happy thoughts.

I'm not bored, or restless. There's nowhere else, my Bobbi, that I'd rather be. You're growing, one heartbeat at a time. Every heartbeat's a triumph in itself.

I feel we're closer than ever — don't you? And your once goal-oriented mom is feeling downright mystical and calm.

It's quiet around here. The TV's off, the phones are on mute. Our bedside phone flashes when someone calls. If we're awake, and caller ID says it's someone we love, we answer.

We talk, of course, you and I. And, for the record, I'm predicting the first full sentence I believe you'll speak. Not the first words, though I believe I know those, too.

Daddy! Daddy! Daddy!

Aunt Meg! Aunt Meg! Aunt Meg!

(And yes, I know you'll say Mommy! Mommy! Mommy! too.)

Your first full *sentence,* will be " 'Twas the night before Christmas" — followed, bright girl, by a recitation of the entire poem.

You know it by heart, don't you? You've heard me say it, and think it, so many times.

It's my mantra, when I need one, when all the determination in the world can't get me back to mystical calm on the occasions — and there are some — when happy thoughts are highjacked by fear.

The mantra does the trick. I see three-year-old Meg curled up beside me, and I see the illustrations we loved.

My search for our girlhood edition of the book came to an unproductive end even before Kathleen took me off-line. I have another plan, on hold except in my head until after you're born. Although, thanks to our mantra, my image of the storybook colonial is becoming ever more clear.

I'll do a design of it, as if I was designing any other home, and send the JPEG to a woman in Oregon, in a place called Sarah's Orchard, a client told me about. She'll make a needlepoint of it, in any size I like. I'm thinking pillow-size. I know, a pillow for Meg feels like coals to Newcastle. Not that I've seen any evidence that she makes pillows for herself.

She's making pillows for you, though. And an entire kingdom of stuffed animals.

The needlepoint pillow will make a nice Christmas present, I think. Your very first Christmas gift for Aunt Meg.

Caroline allowed herself a future image, a calming one. This coming Christmas, Bobbi's first, in their Keswick Drive home. It was only the five of them, the sisters, the men they loved, their precious baby girl. Jeffrey's family, including Bobbi's namesake, were on their way from Denver, but had yet to arrive.

After a smiling moment, she reminded herself of a more immediate — happy — future.

Your dad's delivering his closing arguments even as I'm writing to you. The defense scored a few points, he says, during their case. But he's optimistic that once the jury reviews all the evidence, they'll vote to convict.

He's expecting a lengthy deliberation, as he feels it should be. Finding a man guilty of double homicide feels far weightier and requires more time than setting him free.

Meg, by the way, insists that Marteen scored *no* points, and that the guilty verdict is a "done deal" even before your dad gives his closing.

The jury should have the case, and Judge Owens's instructions, by the end of the day. They'll begin their deliberations tomorrow. The best part is that your dad will have a chance to rest, to breathe, to take long naps with us. And spend every minute of the weekend at home.

He'll go to the office tomorrow, to clear his desk — and to be in the vicinity of the courthouse in the event of jury requests for transcript read backs. He's decided that, between three and four tomorrow, "in the vicinity of" will include Kathleen's office for our weekly visit.

Meg will drive us, and he'll meet us there.

He'll get to watch while Kathleen documents how much, despite this preeclampsia, you've continued to grow.

Please, Caroline thought. Please let that be what Kathleen finds.

As the thought began to veer toward terror, she whispered to herself and to her daughter, " 'Twas the night before Christmas . . ."

Chapter
Twenty-Nine

Friday, July 29
7:00 a.m.

"Good morning." Mark, dressed for work, kissed her sleepy face. "Again."

Meg smiled at the reminder of the way they'd greeted each other an hour ago.

"Good morning again." She touched the diamond ring he'd given her late last night. "It's so beautiful, Mark."

"You're so beautiful."

"It's also . . . grand. Far grander than I —"

"Don't say deserve."

"How about need?"

"No good, either. You have to tell me you don't want it, Meg, or that you want something else. Otherwise, it stays where it is."

"I don't want anything else." She touched his face. "And I defy anyone to even try to get this ring off my finger."

"That's better." Mark kissed her hand as he spoke. "Caroline's appointment's at three?"

"Yes. I'll probably head over to her house about one-thirty. I have this very grand ring, and the very grand news that comes with it, to share with her. I thought I'd ask her to be my matron of honor. And Bobbi to be our flower girl."

Mark moved a lock of sleep-tousled hair from her suddenly worried eyes.

"Caroline's doing well."

"I know. And the fact that Bobbi's growing as she should be, despite what *has* to be compromised placental blood flow, is remarkable. If everything can just remain this way for another ten days or so, Bobbi will be premature but healthy, and Caroline will be safe."

"Then," he said softly, "ten days it will be. How about making it ten days spent planning a Christmas wedding instead of reading medical texts? You're already a one-woman authority on preeclampsia."

"So much can go wrong."

"Yes, it can. But," Mark repeated, "Caroline is doing well."

Meg nodded. "I know. I *know*. Mark?"

"Yes?"

"Will you take the pink bear with you?

And give it to the little girl whose sister was killed?"

"That's one of Bobbi's bears."

"Bobbi's *many* bears. Too many. In fact, if you think there's a use for them at the medical center, I'd be happy to donate all the stuffed animals I've already made. I can sew more. I've decided to make a new one for Bobbi, a special one. A snowy white bear with silver thread and silver lining." She'd bought the fabric and notions yesterday. Not the most practical color scheme for a baby — she'd make a wardrobe of seasonal outfits, too — but for the Gallagher girls it was the color of bad memories made happy. The color of love. The white-and-silver bear would be finished ten days from now . . . and not a second sooner . . . and it would be tucked beside the just-born Bobbi in the incubator she'd need for a little while in the neo-natal ICU. "She'd want to give the animals I've made to other little boys and girls. She's very generous, like her mom."

"And," Mark said, "like her aunt. I love you, Meg."

"I love you, too."

"Good morning," Jeffrey whispered as he sat, before leaving for work, on Caroline's edge of their bed.

She responded with a dreamy smile. "Is it morning already?"

The round-the-clock darkness of the room in which she and Bobbi slept for hours between happy thoughts gave no clue to the time, or the brightness, of the summer day.

"Seven-thirty."

"Ah," she murmured. "*Early* morning for the ladies of leisure."

"Who I'll see at Kathleen's office at three."

"We'll be there."

"Shall I check your blood pressure before I go?"

"No. I'm too comfy right where I am. I'll check it as usual at nine. Bobbi and I should be fully awake by then."

"Okay. I'll see you at three. Go back to sleep."

"Don't worry, we will."

Jeffrey pressed his lips against her temple and placed a gentle hand on the belly where their daughter lay.

"I love my girls," he said. "Love my girls."

Caroline didn't awaken at nine.

And when she did, at 11:11, it wasn't the end of sleepiness that awakened her, but a pain, a throbbing, in her wedding-ring finger.

The throbbing made sense. The wedding

ring that had been snug throughout her pregnancy — so snug she'd removed her engagement ring months ago — had, overnight, become barely visible within the swollen tissue enveloping it.

What didn't make sense was *why.* Only when Caroline made it from bed to bathroom, a slow motion journey because her legs felt so heavy, did her brain, slow and heavy, too, begin to understand.

She saw herself in the mirror, saw the massive swelling of her body. It was asymmetric, most marked on the side she'd been lying on. The half of her face exposed to Jeffrey would have appeared its normal, sleepy self.

She knew — slowly, vaguely — what the swelling meant . . . and what she had to do. The realization wasn't urgent, and it should have been. Her brain seemed to be floating in edema, the way she was. And, for a very long time, what focus she had was on removing her ring.

It wouldn't come off. Not with ice-cold water, not with liquid soap.

Kathleen would know someone who could deal with it. She'd mention it to Kathleen when she saw her at three.

No, a voice told her.

You need to see Kathleen soon.

Now.

The voice, perhaps of instinct, was insistent.

But still she could not, did not, rush.

Kathleen would want to know her pressure. She'd check it, and her protein, before calling Meg to ask if she could drive her to the medical center earlier than planned.

And, the voice said, you need to call Jeffrey, too.

At 11:28, Judge Owens received the astonishing news. After confirming it to be true, she arranged a conference call with both lead counsels.

Jeffrey, in his office, was easy to reach. Marteen, en route to lunch at Salty's, had to be paged.

Both attorneys assumed the obvious. The jurors had a question.

Neither considered the possibility that what the jury had was a verdict.

"The jury's reached a verdict," Mark said when Meg answered the phone.

"Oh, Mark." She glanced at the clock above her sewing table. She'd been working in serene silence on Bobbi's bear. "Oh, *no!* They found him not guilty."

"The verdict hasn't been read. The news

just broke that it's been reached. They're expecting it'll be announced at about 1:30. It will take that long to get families, cameras, media to the courtroom."

"It's going to be a not-guilty verdict," she moaned. "The jury's been out, what, three hours?"

"Two hours and twenty-eight minutes."

"It's my fault."

"No. Any more than it's Jeffrey's fault — and you know damned well he's blaming himself right about now."

"He *can't* be. He did everything right."

"And you didn't do anything wrong."

"Except have so much to drink that I didn't remember meeting a murderer. It got out, didn't it? Marteen's version somehow made its way to the jury and created reasonable doubt."

"Will Jeffrey have called Caroline?"

"No. And," she said, "he hasn't called me."

"He'll want you to be with her. Not to tell her what's happening but to prevent media — or even well-meaning neighbors — from showing up at her door."

"I'd better get going."

"I wish I could go with you."

"You can't."

"No. I'll be in my on-call room, keeping the direct line open for you."

"Okay."

"Meg? Not your fault."

"I wish that was true."

CHAPTER THIRTY

Keswick Drive
12:22 p.m.

Something was wrong with the blood pressure cuff. She couldn't fit it around her arm, not the way she was supposed to.

Her arm was swollen, that was why. She'd need a larger cuff to get a valid reading.

Kathleen would have a larger cuff. The sooner she got to Kathleen's office, the sooner the result would be known.

Her pressure would be up.

"It's time," she murmured to Bobbi, "for us to go the hospital. We'll spend the weeks before your delivery there. It'll be fine. We'll be fine. A change of venue, that's all. I'll get us organized, then call Meg."

There wasn't much to get organized. Her suitcase, packed by Meg, was downstairs and ready to go. Also thanks to Meg, there was a closetful of attractive pregnant-mom tops and slacks.

But maybe she should go from home to hospital in her nightgown and robe. Less time out of bed in both places — and more time to write the note she was beginning to realize she needed to write.

She'd better do that now, while she remembered it.

Then call Meg.

She'd write the note in her journal, she decided. She'd be taking the journal with her. She had weeks and weeks of entries to write before Bobbi was born, and it was easier than walking down the hallway to her office — and faster, too, since she was moving so slowly — and searching for a pen and paper there.

Her journal was on her nightstand. All she had to do was turn on the bedside lamp. The knob was simple to twist . . . had been simple.

For some reason she was having trouble grasping it today.

Caroline saw the reason when, at last, the light was on. Her right hand was swollen, too. More swollen than when she'd used it to try prying the ring off her left. Her ring finger was discolored now, purplish. But, she noted idly, it no longer hurt.

Grasping the lamp knob had been difficult. Holding the pen was harder. But critical.

The words she needed to write had to be legible.

She squeezed her fingers so tightly around the pen that it made indentations in the swollen flesh.

Jeffrey,

It's too early for our Bobbi to be born. She has to remain within me as long as it's safe *for her.*

My condition doesn't matter.

Make no decisions based on my welfare.

This is my wish, my darling, and my will.

I trust you to honor it, and to love our baby girl as you've loved me — and as I love you.

Caroline

She closed the journal, the pen inside, and, after trying without success to turn off the light, she stood.

And whirled.

"The whirlies," she murmured as she steadied herself.

Her voice was soft, loving, as her thoughts floated back to the early proof that her baby girl had come to stay.

We see this, Kathleen had said. Hormones.

And when dizziness occurred in pre-eclampsia?

"We'd better get going, my sweet Bobbi. Mommy needs to get us to the hospital . . . now."

"Thirty-eight minutes till verdict time," the radio personality and popular afternoon talk-show host announced as Meg turned off Windermere Road onto Keswick Drive. "And our unscientific poll is getting curiouser and curiouser. The overwhelming majority of those of you who've responded believe Kevin Beale is guilty of the double murders with which he's been charged. But in virtually the same numbers, you're predicting the jury's going to set him free. That's the conventional wisdom. Think O.J. A quick verdict means the jury was unanimous on its first vote. That favors acquittal, the legal eagles say."

"Like we don't know that," Meg snapped, shutting off the radio as she pulled into the drive.

There was nary a reporter standing on the lawn or lurking in the bushes and, if Caroline's neighbors were home, they were all glued to their own TVs.

The master-bedroom curtains were closed, as they should be. It would be possible, Meg decided, to keep Caroline in a news blackout until after her three o'clock appointment with Kathleen. The most important news of the day would be Bobbi's continued growth and development.

Jeffrey could reveal the less important — though devastating — news when he drove Caroline home.

Meg let herself in and, shoes removed for extra stealth, made her way to the staircase that led to the bedroom. She expected to find her sister there, still asleep.

That wasn't where Meg found her.

Caroline was on the stairs, facing the stairs, as she slowly, cautiously, made her way down.

Caroline wasn't crawling. She couldn't crawl. Her bathrobe, hiked to her waist so she wouldn't trip, revealed massively swollen legs that wouldn't bend at the knee.

It was a stiff-legged descent, awkward and unbalanced, and painstaking in her effort not to slip, not to fall, to protect Bobbi above all else.

Meg's slender legs bent just fine, although they trembled as she climbed the stairs.

"Caroline?" Meg said when she was close enough to catch her sister should the sound of her voice startle Caroline into losing what precarious balance she had.

"Meg?"

"Yep. It's me. Right behind you." Meg

placed a gentle hand on a naked thigh. "Hello."

"Hello. I'm glad you're here."

"Me, too. Your legs are swollen."

"I know. I think I should go to the hospital."

Meg's heart screamed as her mind filled with a collage of the worst complications of preeclampsia. It was a visual collage. The textbooks had photographs of ruptured livers and blood-filled brains.

"I think so, too. Let's get you downstairs. I'll guide you, okay?"

"Yes. Thank you."

Don't thank me! "Actually, if you're all right where you are for the moment, I'll call 911."

Meg expected a protest.

She didn't get one.

Caroline's voice might be slow and dreamy, and she'd said, as if it was the most casual of afterthoughts, *I think I should go to the hospital.* But at some level, she understood the seriousness of what was happening.

At some level. Caroline *was* confused — a frightening harbinger, Meg knew, of what might come. All would be lost — Bobbi *and* Caroline — if Caroline had an eclamptic seizure in the passenger seat of Meg's car.

Meg's hand remained on Caroline's leg, her body braced to block a fall while she spoke urgently to the 911 operator who'd dispatch Medic One. The call complete, they began their descent. It was slow, one swollen foot at a time — moved, positioned, held steady by Meg.

When they reached the bottom of the staircase, Caroline turned around with Meg's help. Ever gracious, she smiled.

And squinted at the sunlight in the windowed foyer.

"Is the light bothering your eyes?" Meg asked. *Please say no.*

"A little, I guess. It's more of a flickering."

No. "Let's get you on the living-room couch."

It was a short walk . . . that took forever.

Once on the couch, Caroline, squinting anew, whispered, *"Meg."*

No! "What is it, Caroline?"

"You're wearing a diamond engagement ring."

"Yes. You're going to be my matron of honor," Meg said. "And Bobbi's going to be our flower girl." Meg heard the decisiveness that was a symptom of her own rising fear, and saw how it registered in her sister's struggling brain: as harshness, which confused Caroline all the more. Forcing calm, and letting love surface above terror, Meg said, "Would that be okay with the two of you?"

"We'd be delighted. Thank —"

"Does your head hurt, Caroline?" *Please no, please no, please no* —

"Yes."

CHAPTER
THIRTY-ONE

"Have you reached a verdict?"

"We have, Your Honor."

"Please give your verdict form to the clerk."

The cameras followed every footfall. The clerk walked first to the forewoman. Then the folded sheet of paper was handed off to the judge.

Whose expression, as she scanned the verdict form, was difficult to interpret.

After an inscrutable moment, she returned it to the clerk to be read aloud. Before he did, the defendant and his counsel rose to their feet.

"In the matter of The People of the State of Washington versus Defendant Kevin Beale, we the jury find as follows. In count one, murder in the first degree, the defendant is —"

Mark answered his call-room phone in mid-ring. He knew who it would be, and believed he knew why she was calling.

"Hello, Meg."

"I need you, Mark. Caroline needs you."

"Tell me."

He listened as she did, offering reassurance. "You've done exactly the right thing. Exactly." And posing questions to the one-woman authority on preeclampsia Meg had become.

Mark had become an authority, too, catching up on the literature — it wasn't his field — since he'd studied the topic. Not his field, but not as foreign, either, as it might have been. Twice, as a trauma surgeon, he'd been asked, too late, to scrub in on pre-eclamptic women with shattered livers . . . surgeries he'd chosen not to mention to Meg.

He listened as Meg described the signs and symptoms she'd observed in Caroline. Confusion. Visual disturbance. Headache. Edema.

"Abdominal pain?" he asked. Shattering liver?

"She says no. Mark? Could you hold on a minute? There's something Caroline wants me to see."

"I'm not going anywhere."

"I am," Meg said. "It's actually something

she wants me to get. Her journal. It's upstairs. I'm going there now. At the top of the stairs, she says. I've found it, Caroline! I'm heading back down . . . am back down. She's beckoning to me. She wants me to . . . Inside? Okay. Where the pen is . . . Got it. Read it? All right."

Mark listened to silence as Meg read. To silence, and in silence. In the background, on the call-room TV, the closed captioning that appeared whenever the sound was muted provided an immediate transcript of Judge Owens's words. The verdict on the second count having been rendered, she was thanking the jurors for their service and telling them they could talk to the media, or not. It was up to them.

The silence — in the colonial on Keswick — ended with a difficult exchange.

"It's what I want, Meg."

"She'd be premature, Caroline, but not *that* premature. She's been growing so well."

"She needs to keep growing."

"You don't understand!"

"Yes, Meg. I do. I know I'm a little . . . foggy. But I'm clear on this. Please tell me *you* understand."

"I do, Caroline. But when your pressure goes up, it might be best for the baby if she was delivered."

Mark heard the care and calm with which Meg phrased the medical reality that was haunting her. As Caroline's pressure soared, her vessels further constricting, blood supply to the placenta became severely constricted, too. Emergency delivery could be as life-saving for the baby as it was for the mom.

And delays could be as disastrous.

"Might be," Caroline repeated. "But unless it *is* best for Bobbi — for Bobbi, Meg — I want to wait. Promise me Jeffrey and Kathleen will know that."

"I promise."

"Promise me something else?"

In the instants before Meg's reply, Mark noted, as Meg surely did, the change in Caroline's voice. Having focused every ounce of concentration she could muster until Meg agreed to convey her wishes to Jeffrey and Kathleen, she surrendered — again — to dreaminess. Mark recognized that her determined focus had been an act of will. And of love. An emotional clarity, not a medical one.

"Of course I will," Meg replied. Her voice, too, was changed.

"Will you read the journal?"

"I'd love to, Caroline."

"And read it to Bobbi?"

"*You'll* read it to her," Meg said.

"Remember when I used to read to you?"

"I think about it all the time."

"Read to Bobbi. Will you? Find a copy of *A Visit from St. Nick,* one with illustrations, to read to her. I've tried to find one like ours — do you remember it, Meg? — but I can't."

"*I* can. I know where ours is. I've kept it all these years. We'll all snuggle in bed this Christmas Eve, you, Bobbi, me and — *oh.* Hear that, Caroline?"

"Sleigh bells?"

"No," Meg whispered. *Oh, Caroline.* "Even better. Sirens. Medic One. Stay here while I go outside and direct the paramedics" — *quickly!* — "to you."

As she hurried out the door and onto the front walkway, she spoke to Mark.

"I'm so afraid."

"I know."

"Will you meet us in the ER?"

"You know I will."

"I told the 911 operator Kathleen was Caroline's doctor, but . . ."

"I'll get in touch with Kathleen."

"And Jeffrey?"

"And Jeffrey."

"She doesn't want Bobbi delivered yet."

"So I gather."

"She *has* to. Doesn't she?"

That was the conventional wisdom. Caroline needed to deliver Bobbi. Now. *Five minutes ago.* For Caroline's survival — and, in all likelihood, Bobbi's, too.

But Mark had practiced medicine long enough to know there were always shades of gray. And, sometimes, there were miracles.

"We'll see, Meg. The paramedics will get her here, and Kathleen will assess her status."

"Can you do something for Caroline?"

He'd already planned to offer what technical assistance he could. He'd started an intravenous line last August, when Caroline's blood pressure had been perilously low. If need be, he'd start one in a perilously hypertensive Caroline today.

"Anything."

"Her wedding ring needs to be removed. Cut off. Could you do that?"

Any emergency-room staff member could do it. The procedure that was both straightforward and routine.

It would be straightforward in Caroline — despite the swelling.

But the removal of the symbol of Caroline's undying love for Jeffrey was far from routine.

Meg was trusting Mark to remove Caroline's wedding band reverently.

Her trust went farther. Too far. She was assigning the physician she loved an omnipotence he didn't possess — the power to promise a future in which the ring would glint in sunlight as Caroline, with her healthy Bobbi, admired the springtime garden they'd planted in the fall.

"Mark?"

"I'll remove her ring, Meg." And I'll love you through whatever lies ahead.

CHAPTER THIRTY-TWO

Queen Anne Medical Center
Trauma Room Eight
2:28 p.m.

"Jeffrey." Meg walked toward him as he neared the trauma center entrance. When she saw his face, the worry beyond words, she curled her fist more tightly around the wedding ring in her palm.

She'd keep it safe, for both Caroline and Jeffrey.

"Where is she?"

"Through here." Meg led the way. "Kathleen's examining her. Mark — and others — are also there."

"But they'll be doing the C-section soon."

"I don't know, Jeffrey. Caroline doesn't want them to deliver Bobbi."

"They *have* to. If Caroline's in trouble, Bobbi is, too."

"I don't —"

"Know it's true? You do, Meg. And so do I. You're not the only one who's been reading Williams's *Obstetrics*."

She should have known, and now her mind's eye saw him, in his office, late at night, reading about the condition that could steal his wife, his daughter. His world.

Reading, and looking at the black-and-white photographs of death. The postmortem shots of maternal livers, maternal brains were only the beginning. Babies were pictured, too. Babies, of preeclampsia, who had died. These were as disturbing for a father to view, for anyone to view, as the postmortem photographs of baby Matthew that Jeffrey had declined to show the jury.

Jeffrey had seen the photographs. Of baby Matthew. Of babies who could be his Bobbi.

He'd viewed them alone, at night, in his office. And for Caroline's sake, he'd kept his fear, his terror, to himself.

The woman with whom Jeffrey might have shared his worry was the woman from whom he needed to hide it most.

I've had Mark, Meg thought. He's looked at the photographs with me and held me when I trembled. But Jeffrey's been alone. I should have known it and reached out to him.

"Jeffrey?"

He wasn't listening. They'd arrived at Trauma Room Eight. His mind was on his wife and daughter.

And, Meg discovered when she heard the words Jeffrey whispered, on blaming himself for what had befallen them.

"I should've taken her pressure before I left. Why didn't I?"

Kathleen and Mark emerged from the trauma room just as Meg and Jeffrey were about to enter.

"Let's talk over here." Kathleen gestured to an alcove in the hallway. "She's not alone, Jeffrey. The physicians and nurses with her are doing what I need them to do."

"Preparing her for the C-section."

"Getting her ready to transport to the ICU. I'd expected to be taking her to the OR. Before we got the monitor on Bobbi, I thought an emergency C-section would be the only option — for both of them. But it's not the case. Our placental perfusion measurements are good. The blood supply to Bobbi isn't compromised. If it begins to become compromised, we can deliver her before it's a problem. Bobbi's fine, Jeffrey. I can't tell you why, only that she is."

"And Caroline?"

"If it weren't for her wishes, I'd have

delivered her already. I've told her that. And although she's groggy, I have no doubt she understands. I explained to her that if she delivered today, Bobbi's chances are very good. I'm not talking about survival. At this gestational age, with the neonatal care we have, survival's not a huge concern. But for any preemie, there can be complications — as Caroline knows. She also knows that with each passing day in utero, Bobbi's overall chances improve. It's actually each passing *hour* at this stage. Bobbi's on the cusp of being born early but, in essence, mature. I've ordered intravenous medications that might safely move the maturation process along."

"Will you be able to tell when she's mature enough?"

"I think so," Kathleen replied. "There are a variety of measurements we can do. We'll do them all. When they indicate it's time, I'd hope to deliver her right away."

"You'd hope," Jeffrey repeated.

"Caroline would have to consent. Unless," Kathleen said quietly, "she's unable to give consent a day, three days, a week from now. You need to know where we are, how very dangerous this is for Caroline."

Kathleen wasn't speaking to Mark. The trauma surgeon was completely aware of the life-threatening situation in which Caroline had insisted on being placed.

As Kathleen spoke, she saw that the peril was equally clear to Caroline's husband and sister.

"What can you do for Caroline?" Meg asked. Then said, "Lower her blood pressure?"

"Yes. To the extent we can. Which may not be much. She needs the elevated pressure to provide blood flow to her own vital organs as well as the placenta. We'll also medicate her to minimize — again, to the extent we can — her chance of an eclamptic seizure. It'll have the positive effect of keeping her calm. And, I hope, making her sleep."

"Can I be with her?"

"Of course, Jeffrey. You're welcome anytime." Kathleen punctuated the invitation with a smile. "Having said that, though, I must ask you not to talk to Caroline unless she's fully awake. If she could sleep, quite literally around the clock, that would be ideal. With the medication I'll be giving her, it's possible she can. You're welcome to be with her," Kathleen reiterated. "Anytime. But Caroline will be sleeping, and you need to, as well. Quality sleep. In a bed, not a chair. Caroline won't be alarmed if she awakens and you're not here. She'll be so groggy she won't even know. And, in minutes, she'll fall back to sleep . . . where I want her to be."

"I'll do whatever's best for Caroline."

"I know."

"May I see her now?"

"Absolutely."

Chapter
Thirty-Three

Intensive Care Unit
Queen Anne Medical Center
Friday, July 29
11:47 p.m.

"Quit doing that" Mark said as he approached Kathleen Collier outside Caroline's glass-walled cubicle in the Med-Surg ICU.

Both surgically trained physicians wore scrubs. She'd just delivered a healthy baby boy. Mark had just completed a subtotal splenectomy on a water-skier who, having miscalculated his speed for a dry landing, had collided with a dock.

"Quit doing what, Mark?"

"Beating yourself up."

"Not likely."

"I figured as much. In that case, join the club."

"Why would *you* feel guilty?"

"I was with Meg when she visited Caroline at nine last night. Caroline looked terrific, as good as I'd seen her since the preeclampsia was diagnosed. She was thinking clearly. Her pressure was steady, the same as it'd been all week. I didn't examine her feet, didn't examine *her,* but her face, hands, forearms showed no swelling."

"You couldn't see what wasn't there, Dr. Traynor, much less anticipate what was going to happen overnight."

"But you could have, Dr. Collier? Have you ever seen preeclampsia progress this dramatically before?"

"No, and no. But obviously it can. And did. I should've hospitalized her."

"Her pressure elevation might have been detected several hours earlier if you had. But we'd still be standing right here. Caroline wouldn't have consented to delivery. You'd have lowered her pressure to the level you've been able to safely lower it now. She'd have been on the anti-epilectic sooner, but since she hasn't had a seizure, and didn't have one before you started the meds, that's of no consequence. Caroline did very well at home. I doubt she'd have done as well for as long if you'd hospitalized her."

"That's certainly the decision I made, and

kept making, every time I saw her."

"The right decision, Kathleen."

"Thanks, Mark. And nice try."

"You're not going to quit blaming yourself, are you?" Mark knew the answer. Kathleen wasn't going to stop second-guessing the judgments she'd made, no matter how sound and how careful they'd been. Nor would she stop berating herself for failing to see the unseeable.

"Are you?" Kathleen countered, knowing the answer, his answer, too.

"Not anytime soon."

"You should, though."

"So should you. And," Mark said, "so should Jeffrey."

"You've told him what you just told me?"

"Repeatedly. He hears it, and he'd use the same arguments to reassure us, but he can't let it go, either."

"Do you think he really understands what's happening?"

"That Caroline's chance for survival goes down with every second Bobbi remains inside her? Yes," Mark said. "He understands that."

Kathleen drew a breath. "At least he's gone home. He looked so exhausted. I hope he can sleep."

"If he can, it'll be in my on-call room.

That's as far as I could persuade him to go."

"Then where's Meg?"

"She went home. Without persuasion. She had to find a book for Caroline, and she had some sewing she wanted to do — for Caroline, too. And that," Mark said softly, "was after taking Caroline's ring to a jeweler for repair. She knows Caroline will be asking for it as soon as the swelling goes down."

"So she doesn't understand."

"Yes, Kathleen, she does. She's simply doing what the three of us can't. Believing in a happy ending."

It was an authentic belief, Mark thought. Meg was a true believer. She'd even pointed out to him, as if it was the most conclusive of signs, that his blind cut through Caroline's wedding ring severed none of its engraved words of love. No re-engraving would be required. A little soldering was all it would take to make the ring as good as new.

As Caroline would be, Meg had said. As Caroline *would* be.

Dear Bobbi,

It's Aunt Meg, writing in your mom's journal. It's after midnight, and I'm taking a break to write to you before putting the finishing touches on the fluffy creature you'll come to know as Mr. Bear (or any other name you please!).

I'd planned to finish him in a week or so. But your mom needs him now. I'll give him to both of you in the morning. He'll be tucked safely in her arms, while you're tucked safely inside her.

She loves you so much. You know that, feel that, hear that already. And soon you'll know her love, feel it, hear it in person — mommy to her baby girl.

You miss her happy voice, don't you? Her in-love-with-Bobbi voice.

I miss it, too, Bobbi.

It's only been a few hours. But the absence of her voice is (oops! No cross-outs in your journal, your mom says. No editing, either.) *was* an aching grief. We know it's necessary, don't we? She has to be silent now, sleeping, so she'll be able to chatter morning, noon and night once you're born.

That's what's going to happen, Bobbi. She'll be so excited to see you.

Your mom is courageous. And strong. She's made this choice because it's what she wants to do.

Your dad's courageous, too, and just as strong. It takes great courage, and great strength, to honor the choice your mom has made. He's honoring it, Bobbi, honoring your mom, and loving her, and trusting her. He knows, deep down, that if he'd been in your mom's position, it's the same choice he would've made.

He's not in her position.

But he'd give his life to trade places with her if he could.

The good news is you're going to get to know both of your parents *very* well . . . and for a *very long* time.

And when your three strong personalities clash — which they will, despite the love — you can come grumbling to your Aunt Meg and Uncle Mark.

What fun we're going to have, *all* of us, loving you, little Bobbi, and watching you grow.

CHAPTER
THIRTY-FOUR

Queen Anne Medical Center
Saturday, July 30
7:30 a.m.

As she and Mr. Bear neared the hospital entrance, Meg glimpsed a newspaper headline in a vending machine.

The single-word headline was hard to miss. It spanned the width of the page and stretched down to the fold.

GUILTY!

Meg was digging into her purse for coins when a nurse passing by made further searching unnecessary.

"Isn't it great?" the nurse said. "We were all so afraid a quick verdict meant not guilty."

"So this headline *is* about Kevin Beale?" Meg asked.

"Who else?"

"The jury found him guilty of murdering

Susannah?"

"And Matthew. I can't believe you hadn't heard."

I've been listening for something else, Meg thought as she and Mr. Bear resumed their journey to the ICU. The only news that matters.

My sister's happy voice.

My niece's healthy gurgles.

Listening . . . and in the silent world of no radio and no TV, I've been hearing those glorious sounds.

Jeffrey was alone in Caroline's room.

Alone *with* Caroline, Meg realized as she approached.

Her brother-in-law neither needed nor wanted solace from others.

And since Caroline was going to be fine, Meg reminded herself, he never would.

"Jeffrey," she whispered.

He rose, crossed to the doorway where she stood, and, although it was unnecessary, whispered, too.

"Is she sleeping?"

"Yes."

"How is she?"

"Stable."

It was the truth. Nothing measurable had changed.

But both Meg and Jeffrey knew it was also a lie.

Every heartful of blood that gave life to Bobbi caused damage to Caroline. Her injured cells had yet to release their enzymes and clotting factors into her bloodstream, their tiny membranes holding the destruction within as fiercely as Caroline's body held her baby within.

Against all odds, Bobbi was protected from the relentless pummeling. Caroline was not. The assault was taking its toll. How grave the price would be remained to be seen.

"Good," Meg said, despite that. "And Bobbi?"

"Kathleen thinks the steroids may already be helping her lungs mature."

"That's wonderful." It was. Pure truth. "When will she know?"

"Later this morning."

Hang on, Caroline. Please hang on. "Jeffrey?"

"Yes?"

"I just saw the most interesting headline. *Guilty.*"

"You didn't know?"

Meg shook her head. "The verdict hadn't been announced by the time I got to your house."

But, she thought, it was announced some time before Jeffrey learned what had happened to Caroline.

Meg imagined how those minutes must have felt to him. Relief, and elation and, above all, an eagerness to share the news with Caroline. He'd have known it would be a while before he could drive home to her, and if she didn't guess it the instant she saw the jubilation in his eyes, he'd speak the single word.

He'd have a final, quiet meeting with Susannah's family first; a delay that he and Caroline would embrace, not begrudge. A postverdict conversation with his team was similarly important. And, if they agreed to it, so was a discussion with the jury. Followed by a last press conference.

Jeffrey would be so ready, by the time that press conference rolled around, to be with his wife.

Meg had no idea where he'd been in the after-verdict ritual when Sheila Eitner gave him the message from Mark. He'd rushed by cab from the courthouse steps directly to Trauma Room Eight.

Whatever he was doing, he'd been thinking about Caroline, counting the minutes till he could go home to her, oblivious to the fact that she wasn't even there.

"Does Caroline know?" Meg asked.

"The verdict? I guess not." Jeffrey's shrug said the rest. How inconsequential it had become.

Meg agreed. And yet . . . "I think you should tell her, Jeffrey. She'll want to know. It'll make her happy to know."

Happy.

"I will," he said. "As soon as she wakes up."

Two hours later, Kathleen planned to awaken her patient, prior to taking her to the operating room.

"Bobbi's ready," she explained to Jeffrey and Meg. "I didn't expect it to happen this quickly, but every measurement we've done tells us it has."

"So you'll be doing the C-section," Mark commented as, off-call and signed-out, he entered the room.

"Yes."

"When?"

"Within the hour. Once the teams are in place."

"Teams?" Jeffrey asked.

"A doctor and two nurses from the neonatal ICU, our obstetrical anesthesiologist and another anesthesiologist, Rachel Blair."

Kathleen didn't look at Mark — or Meg

— as she named the woman Mark had dated before Meg . . . and who specialized in anesthesiology for the critically injured.

"Trauma anesthesia," Meg murmured as terrifying complications of preeclampsia echoed in her brain. *Hepatic rupture. Catastrophic bleeding.* The sort of traumatic injuries Rachel Blair was trained to manage.

Meg kept the fearsome complications unsaid, and wished, for Jeffrey's sake, that she'd imposed the same restraint with *trauma anesthesia.*

A glance at him told her it wouldn't have mattered. Jeffrey knew, without a word from her.

He knew.

"Yes," Kathleen said. "I've asked Rachel to be there as a precaution."

"Have you asked any trauma surgeons to scrub in?" Mark asked.

"I was going to, again as a precaution. You were on call last night."

"It was pretty quiet after midnight. I got some rest." Mark didn't elaborate where — at Caroline's bedside — or when . . . until Jeffrey, who'd tried to sleep but couldn't, appeared at 3:00 a.m. Mark hadn't slept, either. But he *had* rested, a downshifting into neutral that left him refreshed and alert. "I'm good to go, Kathleen."

"Okay." Kathleen addressed Jeffrey and Meg. "There's a private waiting area adjacent to the operating room."

Dr. Collier didn't need to clarify why that was where she wanted them to wait. Caroline's loved ones knew that, on occasion, relatives were permitted in the O.R. when a C-section was performed. When the surgery was elective, for example, and both mom and baby were expected to survive.

This wasn't such an occasion.

"The antihypertensive drip has already been slowed. We'll use a different medication during surgery. As she's weaned off this one, she should become less groggy, easier to awaken, if you'd like to talk to her."

One last time.

Jeffrey alone had a chance to talk to Caroline before she was wheeled away.

It was only then, and only briefly, that she opened her eyes.

"Caroline," he whispered.

"Jeffrey. So . . . tired."

"I know you're tired, darling. But Bobbi's ready to be born. It's safe now. And you'll feel so much —"

"No."

"Caroline, it's safe. Bobbi's ready."

"I meant, no, you're tired."

"I'm fine."

"Tired," she insisted.

"A little," Jeffrey conceded as her eyelids fluttered closed. His lips touched the corners of her eyes. "We got him," he said. "The jury convicted on both counts. We did it, my love. It wouldn't have happened without you. You're the reason I fought so hard for Susannah and Matthew. My love for you. My love for you, Caroline. And for our baby. *I love you.*"

The gurney was moving. He had to let her go.

As he drew away, he saw, through tears, her beloved face.

And, on her lips, a most remarkable smile.

Dreamy.

But very determined.

CHAPTER
THIRTY-FIVE

It was too soon, Meg thought when, a mere twenty-one minutes after an O.R. nurse popped in to say the surgery was about to begin, the waiting-area door swung open.

Mark. Wearing royal-blue scrubs, unspattered with blood, and a smile.

The news was good.

His way of announcing it was unexpected.

"Kathleen Collier is one helluva surgeon. She was in and out before Caroline's pressure had a chance to react."

"Out?" Meg asked.

"Kathleen's closing now. Given her speed and economy of motion, she's probably finished." Mark met Jeffrey's tired eyes . . . and saw, very deep, a glimmer of hope. "She'll accompany Caroline back to the unit and meet us there. It'll take awhile. Plenty of time for us to make a slight detour on the way, to see one extremely healthy baby girl."

"Bobbi's fine?" Meg posed the question for her brother-in-law. Jeffrey's voice, or maybe his heart, was dogged with emotion.

"Bobbi's great," Mark replied. "Impressive lungs. Star-quality APGARs. And did I mention beautiful? The neonatology team had very little to do but admire her. They're admitting her to the NICU, but it's everyone's best guess that she'll be transferred to the Newborn Nursery within a week."

Bobbi flourished, and kept flourishing.

Caroline flourished, too. On paper.

Her pressure fell on its own, a drifting to the nice, low level she'd always enjoyed. Her cells, sensing the end of their battering and the presence of oxygenated blood nearby, let go of the toxic factors they'd been hoarding. But, as quickly as the harmful proteins appeared in her bloodstream, they were washed away in the massive tide of edema fluid that, once resorbed, was swiftly excreted.

Caroline looked healthy — on paper. In person, too. Even close up. She was breathing on her own. And, to someone who didn't know, she seemed to be sleeping.

But Caroline was in a place beneath sleep, a level of consciousness from which she couldn't be awakened. As Saturday became

Sunday, then Monday, then Tuesday, it became ever more difficult for medical science to explain why.

A lag in brain recovery was understandable. And common. Of all the body's functional units, the central nervous system was the most intricate and complex. Its internal repairs required extra time.

But . . .

"Good morning!" Meg greeted Caroline early Tuesday.

It was Meg's first visit of the day. Nine hours earlier, she'd told her unresponsive sister, "Good night, Caroline. We'll talk tomorrow."

Now, as she waited for any sign that Caroline had heard her — none — she mentally revised *We'll talk* to *I'll talk.*

She had to shake off her disappointment first, and infuse herself, at least her voice, with undiluted cheer.

"It's been a busy morning already. Mark and I brought in more stuffed animals today. I told you we gave a herd of them to the NICU staff yesterday, for preemies and their families. Today's animals will find homes throughout Pediatrics. That's what Mark's doing now. And Jeffrey, as I'm sure you know, is visiting Bobbi.

"Wait till you see the two of them together,

Caroline." *You have to see them! Please.* "She's as much in love with him as he is with her. You said in your journal that she'd know his voice. She *does.* You can see her excitement. *Wait* till you see it. She's getting to know her Aunt Meg's voice, too. And her Uncle Mark's. But you know what, Caroline? She needs to hear your voice. Her mommy's voice. Sometimes, when I'm holding her and it's quiet, I feel that she's listening for your voice, straining to hear it. Missing it . . . and needing it."

Dammit, Caroline! Do you hear me? Wake up. Please. Meg took a breath. "Here's something else I did since leaving you last night. Don't get mad. You'll be mad enough at me as it is for giving Bobbi a snow-white bear."

Meg touched that bear, curled in the crook of Caroline's now-slender arm. "Remember I told you I had our copy of *A Visit from Saint Nick?* I do, and I've found it. I've been reading it, and looking at the pictures, and thinking about the plan you wrote about in your journal — my needlepoint pillow. I've been reading your journal, too. As you asked to. And rereading it. I love the journal, Caroline, *and* the plan. I want that pillow. But here's what I thought. You're going to be busy planting bulbs, and cleaning

Mr. Bear, and loving your baby girl and adoring husband. Why take time from those important activities to design a drawing I can easily scan? I guess I answered that question for you. You shouldn't. There's no reason to. So. I did scan it. And, since the JPEG looked great, I Googled 'Sarah's Orchard' and 'needlepoint' to see if I could find the lady to send it to. I did. No problem. So, while Mark was loading stuffed creatures in the car, I e-mailed the JPEG to her. I've asked her to make two needlepoint pillows, one for each of us, with the Christmas house on one side and a saying on the other."

A saying I'll recite to you. Sometime. When I can do it without crying. When the emotions get tough . . . Meg took a few breaths this time. Then a few more.

"You've probably seen the saying. 'I smile because I'm your sister. I laugh because there's nothing you can do about it.' Anyway, I hope it's okay, my taking your idea and running with it. If not, you can get mad at me about the pillow *and* Mr. Bear."

Get mad at me about anything, Caroline! Wake up and yell at me if you want. Not that you ever would. Just wake up.

"Jeffrey's picking up your wedding ring this morning. Your finger's been ready since

Sunday. But the ring hasn't been. The jewelry store's gold-soldering guy only comes in after-hours on Monday nights. We've been assured we can have the ring the moment the store opens today. I told Jeffrey I'd get it. But he wants to, Caroline. He said he picked up both your wedding bands the day you were married. He wants to do it again. Did I tell you how much he loves you? You're right. I have, a zillion times. I know he's been telling you, too. No, I have not been eavesdropping. It's just so obvious. It's always been obvious. You have to wake up for him, Caroline. *You have to.* For him, and for Bobbi."

Please.

The jewelry store opened at ten.

At ten forty-five, Jeffrey, alone with his bride, put the ring on her finger.

"I, Jeffrey, take thee, Caroline, to be my wife. And my life. You are. You, and now Bobbi. My wife, Caroline. My *life.* Always."

He held her hand in his. Held it, for if he didn't, it would fall away.

But as he lifted it, holding it, to his lips, it seemed — was it true? — that she was holding him, holding on . . . too.

And, beyond the bands of gold, his and hers, he saw her eyes.

"Caroline." My Caroline.

He moved to those eyes, so near, so dear. And alive for him.

"Jeffrey." My Jeffrey.

Sometime later, not much later, Roberta Margaret Wynn was placed in her mother's arms.

And she was held against her mother's heart.

She snuggled with contentment, in peace, until her mother spoke.

"Bobbi," Caroline whispered. "Precious Bobbi."

The little face looked up, eyes wide, arms moving, her entire being an excited smile.

You were lost, Mommy. *Lost* . . .

But now — Mommy! Mommy! Mommy! — you are found.

EPILOGUE

'Twas the night before Christmas
It was the Yuletide scene Caroline had envisioned. Meg and Mark. Jeffrey and Caroline. And Bobbi. Jeffrey's family would arrive from Denver in the morning.

It was also a wedding scene. A minister stood in the living room, too.

The best man, Jeffrey, held the five-month-old flower girl. Their responsibility, daughter and dad, was to hand Meg's wedding band to Mark at the appropriate time.

The matron of honor, Caroline, held Mr. Bear. In the double-ring ceremony Meg and Mark had chosen, they had responsibilities, too.

Rings were exchanged that Christmas Eve.

And promises were pledged.

And afterward, there was a story to be read. By all of them. All the voices Bobbi loved.

349

It was a special story, from a special book.

For Bobbi, as it had been for the Gallagher sisters when they were girls, there were pictures to treasure — and to pat.

Bobbi patted the brightly colored pictures.

And as they read to her in turn, she patted Mommy's mouth, and Daddy's, then Aunt Meg's and Uncle Mark's.

And far above earth, in a petticoat sky, sleigh bells chimed.

Can you hear them?

Bobbi could.

Snow fell from the sky.

And on that wedding night, a baby, as unique as a snowflake, found within Meg a loving home.

ABOUT THE AUTHOR

Katherine Stone is the bestselling author of more than twenty novels, including *The Cinderella Hour, Another Man's Son* and *The Other Twin.* Her books have been translated into twenty languages worldwide. A physician who now writes full-time, she lives with her husband, novelist Jack Chase, in the Pacific Northwest.